DISASTER DOWNSTAIRS

Just then the Duke of Pelham climbed down from his carriage and listened in amazement to the sounds of merriment coming from his servants' hall. "Probably getting drunk on my wine," he said furiously to Fergus.

He was in a bad mood, caused, had he but realised it, by his own uneasy conscience. For he had been largely responsible for Jenny's social failure. It had made him furious to see her standing there as if expecting homage from everyone who set eyes on her.

He marched into his front parlour and stretched his hand out towards the bell. No! He would confront these servants.

He walked down the backstairs and threw open the door of the servants' hall. Jenny was twirling around in the arms of his butler while the other servants laughed and cheered.

She was the first to see him. She let out a gasp of horror, all happiness and life draining from her face.

"What is the meaning of this?" the Duke demanded...

Also by Marion Chesney

RAINBIRD'S REVENGE

Book 6 of
A House for the Season

MARION CHESNEY

ST. MARTIN'S PRESS/NEW YORK

RAINBIRD'S REVENGE

Copyright © 1988 by Marion Chesney.

Library of Congress Catalog Card Number: 87-27962

ISBN: 0-312-91294-3

Printed in the United States of America

St. Martin's Press hardcover edition published 1988
First St. Martin's Press mass market edition/December 1988

10 9 8 7 6 5 4 3 2 1

For Mr. Albert Sinclair

RAINBIRD'S REVENGE

Chapter One

For ennui is a growth of English root,
Though nameless in our language:—we retort
The fact for words, and let the French translate
That awful yawn which sleep cannot abate.

—Lord Byron

"What do you mean, fellow, by telling me there is no room to be had in this inn?" The landlord of The Bell glanced nervously up at the tall figure on the inn threshold.

"Just like I said, sir. An assembly is being held here tonight, and folks have come from far and wide to attend it. All the rooms are taken, Mr——?"

"John," said the tall gentleman. "Mr. John. Double your price, landlord, if you find me a room. I shall wait in the tap while you go about arranging it."

He strode into the tap with his servant at his heels, leaving the landlord, Mr. Sykes, looking after him open-mouthed.

"What was all that about?" asked his wife, coming up behind him.

"Some gentleman called Mr. John demanding a room. Says he'll pay double."

"Well, could be done," said his wife cautiously. "There's young Mr. Partridge and his friend, Mr. Clough. They'd rack up together at a pinch."

"Don't like this Mr. John's high-handedness, and that's a fact," said the landlord.

"Money's money," said his practical wife. "You know the Assembly Committee won't pay us anything till Martinmas."

"Very well," said the landlord reluctantly. "But you go and tell him he can more than likely have a room. He's in the tap. Something about him makes my flesh creep."

Mrs. Sykes straightened her cap and opened the door of the tap while her husband made his way upstairs.

A few of the locals were looking sulky, as if they had just been ejected from their customary place, at two men who were seated in the best chairs in front of the fire.

Mrs. Sykes was perfectly prepared to give the strangers a piece of her mind and tell them they were very lucky indeed if they could get a room, double fee or no double fee; but, at her approach, the taller of the two men rose to his feet, and the angry words died on her lips.

A pair of ice-blue eyes in a tanned face looked down at her haughtily from above the snowy folds of an exquisitely tied cravat. His hair was the colour of burnished guineas. His mouth was firm and classically shaped. He exuded an air of wealth and power. Mrs. Sykes sank into a curtsy.

"My husband has gone to see if two of our guests will agree to share a room," she said. "That will leave a room free for you, sir and . . . ?" She looked inquiringly at the smaller man.

"For my servant," said the tall man. "Thank you. You are most kind." He smiled suddenly, a smile of dazzling sweetness that was suddenly at odds with his chilly grandeur.

"And if your honour would care to grace our ball," said Mrs. Sykes, feeling breathless after the impact of that smile, "I am sure the Assembly Committee would be most honoured."

The tall man surveyed her thoughtfully. "Perhaps," he said. "We shall see. Please let me know as soon as the room is ready."

Mrs. Sykes curtsied again and left.

The two men sat down. "Well, Fergus," said the tall man, "shall I visit this rustic ball?"

"If it amuses your grace," said his servant. "But why the masquerade? Why not tell the landlord you are the great and noble Duke of Pelham?"

"Because I am tired of toad-eaters and fortune hunters," said the duke lazily. "I wish a short holiday from the breed. You know that, Fergus. We have been together for many years now and through many battles. I allow you more licence than anyone else. But if I choose to remain incognito for this one evening, that is my affair."

A flicker of affection lit the duke's eyes as he glanced at the disapproving lines of Fergus's sunburned face: Fergus, once devoted batman, now valet, companion, and sometimes adviser.

"But the servants at that accursed London house know your identity," said Fergus.

"Yes."

"I do not know why your grace should choose to spend the Season at Sixty-seven Clarges Street."

"Because, or had you forgot, my town house in

Grosvenor Square is being redecorated, so I must reside in the lesser of my town properties."

"But your father killed himself there, your grace!"

"We are but lately returned from the wars in the Peninsula, and yet you have managed to listen to gossip about me, Fergus."

"Is it not true?"

"Yes. But I am not sentimental. Nor do I believe in ghosts. I knew little of my father, and the little I knew I did not like. Clarges Street will do very well. Perhaps the delights of the Season will remove some of this ennui that plagues me."

His servant looked at him slyly. "Or perhaps some beauty will take your interest."

The duke sighed. "Women are only interested in money," he said. "They are mercenary to a fault."

"There might be some unspoiled and fresh country beauty at this ball," said Fergus, chatting easily to his employer with the casual friendliness which had developed between master and servant during the bloody campaigns against Napoleon's soldiers.

"Women are spoilt from birth," said the duke. "The subject bores me. Talk about something else."

Miss Jenny Sutherland looked at her own appearance in the glass with extreme satisfaction. It was a pity, she thought, not for the first time, that such beauty should be wasted on the country air. But her aunt, Lady Letitia Colville, who could have well afforded to have taken her to London for a Season, showed absolutely no signs of doing so.

Jenny *was* pretty. Masses of soft dark hair framed a

delicate face. She had large brown eyes with long black lashes, a short straight nose, and a perfect mouth. Her figure was soft and feminine and she had a tiny waist—not often shown to advantage in the latest styles, where the waist had moved up to somewhere just below the bosom.

Her parents had died when she was six years old from the "French cold"—the name for influenza—the French being blamed for any illness, from a cold in the head to the pox. Her spinster aunt, Lady Letitia, had elected to bring her up. Personal beauty, rather than her aunt's upbringing, had spoilt Jenny. She had become used to hearing from an early age from a doting governess how very beautiful she was, so that her aunt's efforts at instilling some modesty in her brain had gone to waste.

She was wearing a dress of silver spider gauze over a white slip. A coronet of white silk flowers and silver ribbons nestled among her curls. Jenny knew she was in no danger of being a wallflower at the assembly that evening. At all previous assemblies she had been the belle of the ball.

Her maid entered carrying a warm shawl, fan, and reticule. Jenny did not like the choice of fan and wanted to send the maid, Cooper, to look for another, but refrained from doing so, for Cooper would report even such a minor task to Lady Letitia, and Lady Letitia would promptly accuse Jenny of giving the servants unnecessary work.

Carrying an oil-lamp, Cooper lit the way downstairs to the drawing room for Jenny. Lady Letitia was sitting by the drawing-room fire.

She was a slim woman in her early forties. Her hair was thick and brown without a trace of grey and her small black eyes were sharp and sparkling. She had a neat, rather flat-chested figure, long white hands, and long, narrow feet encased in kid dancing slippers. She wore a velvet turban and a gown of crimson velvet fastened with gold frogs over an underdress of dull-green silk.

She looked up as Jenny entered the room, wishing again that the girl were not quite so dazzlingly beautiful. Lady Letitia found herself hoping there would be some gentleman at the ball who would catch her flighty niece's fancy—some gentleman who would have no interest in Jenny at all. What she needs, thought Lady Letitia, is a good set-down. It was not as if Jenny were cruel or unkind. It was merely that she had obviously become accustomed to thinking her beauty too great for any of the local gentry. In short, she was vain.

Perhaps I should have taken her to London, mused Lady Letitia. *There are many beauties there, and competition is just what she needs. But London is full of rakes and fribbles. Better with a country husband.*

"How do I look?" asked Jenny, pirouetting in front of her aunt.

"Very suitable," said Lady Letitia repressively.

Jenny laughed. "I can never wring a compliment from you, dear Aunt."

"It is as well there is someone in the world who does not spoil you," said Lady Letitia. "My pelisse, Cooper."

Lady Letitia lived in a large mansion outside the town of Barminster. It was a busy market town, being on the main road from Bristol to London. Although many London-bound strangers often stayed at The Bell, few ever graced the assemblies, being too tired from travelling to think of attending a local ball.

After Jenny had left her shawl in an ante-room and joined her aunt in the hall outside the double doors that led to the ballroom, she began to feel tremors of excitement, as if something momentous were about to happen.

They were somewhat late, vain Jenny deliberately delaying her toilette so that she might make an appearance.

"Good Gad," muttered the Duke of Pelham as Jenny entered the room, followed by Lady Letitia.

"There is your country beauty," murmured Fergus from behind his master's chair. "And what a beauty!"

"I wonder if she is aware of her looks," said the duke, still studying Jenny. But there was nothing in Jenny's manner to betray her vanity, simply because Jenny had never ever had to compete with anyone.

Lady Letitia's sharp eyes immediately flew to where the Duke of Pelham was sitting. She raised her fan and whispered behind it to Mrs. Chudleigh, a member of the Assembly Committee, "Who is that devastatingly handsome stranger?"

"No one of any importance, I can assure you," said Mrs. Chudleigh. "A traveller called Mr. John."

Lady Letitia looked covertly across the room at the handsome, haughty face and murmured, "I am surprised to learn he is a plain 'mister.' I would say he is used to commanding a great number of people."

"Possibly," said Mrs. Chudleigh with a superior titter. "His servant has put it about that his master was an army captain but recently sold out."

Jenny, who had been joined by several of her friends, soon learned the identity of the handsome stranger as well.

"Mama says she will shoot me if I so much as look at a lowly captain," giggled Miss Euphemia Vickers, one of Jenny's friends. "But he is so handsome and has such an air."

As the dance progressed, a feeling of animosity towards the "captain" grew among the guests. For he did not dance. He merely looked curiously at the dancers like an entomologist examining the mating habits of a rare breed of insect.

And then Mr. Sykes, the landlord, sidled up to Mrs. Chudleigh and whispered, "There is a Lord Paul Mannering but lately arrived and desirous to attend the ball."

"A lord!" cried Mrs. Chudleigh. "But of course he has our permission. In fact, I do not even need to consult the other members of the committee."

Mr. Sykes bowed and withdrew. Mrs. Chudleigh flew from one to the other to herald the arrival of this Lord Paul Mannering. Another member of the committee, who studied the Peerage as others might study their Bible, reported that Lord Paul was the youngest son of the old Duke of Inchkin, a widower, and a general in Wellington's army.

As the room buzzed with all this exciting gossip, the Duke of Pelham suddenly rose to his feet and made his way towards Jenny. She saw his coming with alarm. What if this Lord Paul should suddenly appear? It was the supper dance, and she would be tied to this Mr. John—a nobody. Before he could reach her, she slipped away through a group of guests and hid behind a pillar. The duke stood frowning. He was used to young ladies standing rooted to the spot, trembling with anticipation should he deign to approach them. He shrugged and returned to his seat.

"It is the supper dance," muttered Fergus.

"I'll take someone, anyone in, feed, and then go to bed," yawned the duke. "It has been fun watching all these pleasant English people enjoying themselves, but now I am monstrous bored."

8

But he was not precisely bored. He was piqued and irritated by that young beauty who had fled before his advance. He put up his glass and surveyed the line of chaperones. In the past, he had often found one of their number a more entertaining companion to take to supper than any young miss. His eye fell on Lady Letitia and liked what it saw. He rose once more to his feet. At that moment, the doors to the assembly room opened, and Lord Paul Mannering, accompanied by a friend, walked in.

There was a ripple of disappointment among the young ladies who had expected the youngest son of a duke to be . . . well, *young*. But this man was in his early forties at least. His raven-black hair showed traces of grey and his strong, harsh face was burnt dark brown by the sun.

"Pelham!" he cried, his eyes lighting on the duke. "By all that's holy, when did you return?"

"Just before you, I think," smiled the duke. "How did you get a room so easily?"

"Wrote and booked in advance. May I introduce my friend," said Lord Paul. "Pelham, this is Mr. Walker. James, may I present his grace, the Duke of Pelham."

Mrs. Chudleigh, who had been listening avidly to this exchange, nearly fainted with excitement. Feathers dipped and turbans nodded as she spread this startling news about the room. Jenny's face flamed with mortification. A duke! And he had been about to ask her to dance.

"Take your partners for the supper dance, please," said the Master of Ceremonies for the third time—for with all this thrilling gossip, people had quite forgotten to take their places in the sets.

"Now, let me find an agreeable lady," said Lord Paul. "Ah, there is the very one."

Jenny, standing beside Lady Letitia, who was seated, smiled and lazily waved her fan as she saw both men bearing down on her. Which should she choose? Why, the duke, of course. He was the younger and the higher in rank.

Lord Paul bent over Lady Letitia. "Will you do me the honour, ma'am, of dancing with me?"

Jenny let out a mortified little gasp, but there was worse to come.

"I' faith," said the duke, "you have stolen a march on me, for I meant to ask this lady myself."

Lady Letitia looked up at both men in a dazed way.

"But, Pelham," said Lord Paul sweetly, "I asked the lady first."

"So you did," said the duke. "I must content myself with second-best." He looked around the room. He was very tall and his eyes ranged over Jenny's head.

Then, with a resigned little sigh, he lowered them and said to Jenny, "Will you do me the honour, miss?"

Jenny quickly agreed. It was infuriating to be classed as second-best, but then she consoled herself with the thought that both gentlemen had been overly gallant because of her aunt's great years.

There was little opportunity for conversation because it was a country dance, but Jenny did not expect her partners to do much more than to look at her with adoring eyes.

It was brought home to her as she finally sat beside the duke at the supper table that it was not adoration in the eyes that looked into her own, but boredom.

"Who is that stylish lady over there?" asked the duke, waving his gold quizzing glass in Lady Letitia's direction.

"That is my aunt, your grace."

"Does she possess a name?" he ask with a shade of irritation in his voice.

"Yes, your grace. Lady Letitia Colville."

"Ah, the late Earl of Mallock's daughter."

"Yes, your grace. My aunt was my late mother's sister."

"And you are . . . ?"

"Miss Jenny Sutherland, your grace."

"How do you know my title?"

"It was whispered about a moment ago," said Jenny.

He applied himself to his food. Jenny was uncomfortably aware of the duke's servant, standing at attention behind his master's chair. She looked across at her aunt. Whatever Lady Letitia had just said to Lord Paul was amusing that gentleman very much. Jenny saw that her own friends were covertly watching her and realised that this duke was demonstrating to all and sundry that he found the food on his plate much more intriguing than his partner.

"Then if you are not a captain," said Jenny, "you have not been in the wars."

"On the contrary, I am newly returned."

"How goes it with our troops?" asked Jenny, who had not the slightest interest in the war but longed to make it appear to her watching friends as if he were enraptured by her.

He began to talk. Jenny looked down at her gown to make sure it was hanging in the correct folds. She wished she could take out her mirror to assure herself that she was looking as beautiful as ever.

"I am sorry you find my account tedious." The harsh voice of the duke penetrated her thoughts.

"I find it fascinating, sir," said Jenny, her face flaming.

"Then why," said the duke in measured tones, "were you fiddling with your gown and straightening your gloves while I was talking?"

11

The answer to that one was that Jenny had never had to bother about being anything other than beautiful before. "I assure you, sir," she said sharply, "that I was listening to every word."

"So what did you think of my story of Wellington falling from his horse?"

"Vastly interesting."

"I never told any such story," said the duke.

"Really," said Jenny, fanning herself vigorously, "you are determined to take me in dislike."

"Not I. But I dislike rudeness, and you *are* rude. You might do your partner the courtesy of listening to him."

Jenny batted her long eyelashes and flirted with her fan, two manoeuvres that would, she knew from past experiences, have a devastating effect on any man with a heart.

The duke scowled at her and poured himself a glass of wine. The pair surveyed each other in high irritation. They were a perfect match. The duke was used to people hanging on his every word because of his title, and Jenny was accustomed to slavish devotion.

"The trouble with you, miss," said the duke, his eyes wandering down the long table, "is that you consider yourself the queen of this provincial little town. A Season in London would soon put you in your place."

"And what is that place, your grace?"

"Why, that of a little nobody."

"You," said Jenny, "are the *nastiest* man I have ever met. You are pompous and unkind. You are full of ideas of your own importance. No, I shall *not* go to London, and *thank goodness* for that, for if I did, I might have to see your *stupid* face again, and again suffer from your *stupid* uncouth manners."

"If you were a man," said the duke, becoming very angry indeed, "I would call you out."

Jenny rested her chin on her hand and smiled up at him sweetly. "But I am not. Here you are at a country ball and must make the best of it."

His ice-blue eyes glinted. He rose to his feet and walked a little away. "Come, Fergus," he said loudly to his servant, "I find the impertinent company of Miss Jenny highly tedious." And then he walked from the room.

Jenny sat stricken, shaking with the shame of it all.

"Good Heavens!" cried Lord Paul, jumping to his feet. "What has come over Pelham? He is usually the soul of courtesy."

"Sit down, my lord," said Lady Letitia quietly. "One scene is enough this evening, I think."

Lord Paul slowly sat down. "I think you should let me go after him, ma'am," he said, "and demand an apology."

"Wait until later, my lord," said Lady Letitia calmly. "Jenny can be quite infuriating, and she has had her own way with the gentlemen for too long. Only see! She has been joined by young Mr. Partridge. He will pay her fulsome compliments, and she will soon forget about your friend. Let us talk about something else. I gather you are to be in London for the end of the Season?"

Jenny should have been comforted by both Mr. Partridge's compliments and his criticisms of the Duke of Pelham. Had he known, vowed Mr. Partridge, that this duke should prove to be such a lout, then he would never have given up his room to him. Jenny was better off here in the country, with good honest people and where she was not prey to the insults of London dilettantes and rakes.

But Jenny was miserable. Her beauty had saved her from insult or criticism at all times in the past. She felt it crumbling away, leaving her naked and gauche—a country bumpkin with neither wit nor conversation.

Lady Letitia covertly studied her niece's downcast face while listening to Lord Paul's suggestion that she should take Jenny to London for what was left of the Season.

"You may say, ma'am," said Lord Paul, "that your niece is better suited to the quiet ways of the country and that the blandishments of London might turn her head, but would it not be better to expose her to some of them now? What if she should marry some staid country swain who decides to take her to Town one day and finds her head completely turned? What sort of wife would she make then?"

"You are most persuasive, my lord," said Lady Letitia with a laugh. "I shall think it over."

The Duke of Pelham remained in a seething rage as Fergus prepared him for bed. "Your grace appears to have been monstrous put out by that chit," ventured Fergus at last.

The duke said something that sounded like "grummph."

"Not like you to take it so much to heart," went on Fergus doggedly. "Not as if you have any liking for the ladies."

"I am not a misogynist," said the duke with a reluctant smile. "My purpose in visiting the Season is to find a wife."

Fergus nearly dropped the pile of damp towels he was holding.

"A wife! Why?"

"I need heirs," said the duke testily, "and I cannot go about having them by myself."

"Have you really thought about it?" asked Fergus cautiously. "You'll need to woo one of 'em, your grace, and pay 'em pretty compliments."

"Fiddle," said the duke cynically. "When did a rich English duke ever have to put himself out over any female? I simply select one and snap my fingers."

"Unless, of course, the female happens to be someone like Miss Jenny Sutherland," said Fergus slyly.

"Do not mention that creature's name again. Too much puffed up by her own consequence."

"Like some I could name," muttered Fergus.

"Did you say something?"

"No, your grace. Nothing at all."

In the carriage home, Lady Letitia said to Jenny, "I said, I have decided to remove to London. Did you not hear me? Oh, I had forgot. You hardly ever listen to anybody."

"That is not true!" said Jenny hotly. "I was merely taken aback by the suddenness of it all. I have quite decided I would not like to go to London after all."

"You have, have you? Well, on this occassion, miss, I am going to get my own way. Lord Paul Mannering persuaded me I should take you."

"He did?" Jenny sat back and remembered Lord Paul's harsh, handsome face. He was a trifle old, but he was a lord. His interest in her was just as it should be. Jenny's vanity slowly returned, warming her whole body.

"Then of course we must go," she said with a little laugh. "Lord Paul must not be disappointed."

Now, what, wondered Jenny, seeing her aunt's sad shake of the head and infinitesimal shrug, *was there about that remark to offend her?*

Chapter Two

"Are we going straight to Clarges Street, your grace?" asked Fergus, sitting up on the box of his master's travelling carriage beside the duke, who was driving.

"No. I shall call on Palmer at his office in Holborn. I want to look at the books."

"Do you think him dishonest?"

"Perhaps. He seemed strangely reluctant in his letter to allow me to reside in Clarges Street. He appeared shocked and amazed that I had even remembered the place. He told me there is a staff of servants there, as the house is let every Season. He added that as the house had been let for this Season, perhaps I might prefer to put up at an hotel. I told him to evict the tenants—probably very high-handed of me—but he has made me suspicious. He wrote back to say the house was haunted by the ghost of my father. I then wrote to him to tell him not to be such a crass fool and to expect my arrival."

Fergus shivered. "Perhaps it is, your grace."

"Nonsense. Utter nonsense. I am surprised at you, Fergus. My father was a selfish old man, and quite mad. Having successfully quit this world, he certainly would not want to come back into it."

"Perhaps he had no alternative?"

"I refuse to believe in a divine punishment which subjects the soul to haunt a Mayfair town house. Pull yourself together."

Palmer was waiting for them, as he had been waiting, day in and day out, since he had first received the news of the duke's impending arrival. The duke had written to him from Bristol.

Jonas Palmer's heart plummeted as he looked down from the window and saw the Duke of Pelham climbing down from the box of his carriage. He remembered the duke as a slim, pretty youth, more interested in his studies than anything to do with his vast estates. Palmer had not seen him since the duke had gone to the Peninsula to fight for his country. That pretty boy had turned into a tall, commanding figure of a man.

Palmer scuttled behind his desk, opened a ledger and began to write as if sweating over the cares of the duke's estates.

The door opened, and the duke strode in. "Goodness, it's hot in here," he remarked, and, going to the window, jerked it open, then shrugged his driving coat off and tossed it in a corner. He pulled up a chair and faced Palmer.

"Now," said the duke, "out with it."

"I do not understand, your grace. Out with what?"

"I want the reasons why you tried to put me off taking

up residence in Clarges Street. All that fustian about ghosts."

"My lord, I swear it is true," said Jonas Palmer, one fat hand clutching at the region of his heart.

The duke leaned back in his chair and studied the agent from head to toe. Palmer was short and stocky, with a fat, beefy, belligerent face. "You don't," said the duke in a chill voice, "look to me like a man who believes in anything at all spiritual or supernatural."

"People have seen the ghost," said Palmer. "Bad things have happened since the death of your beloved pa——"

"The late Duke of Pelham, to you, sirrah," corrected the duke sharply.

"Since the death of the late duke. A murderer's been taken, a girl killed and—"

"And all because you appear to have been singularly lax in your choice of tenants. If bad things have been happening there, it is not because the house is accursed, but because the people you allowed to inhabit it have loose morals. So we will have no more of your nonsense. Let me see the books."

"I have them here, your grace," said Palmer.

The duke produced a quizzing glass and began to turn over the pages of the ledgers. "I see you have been renting the house for eighty pounds for a Season. Odd's life, man, you could have demanded a thousand!"

"If you ask about, you will find it is not only I who consider the house accursed," said Palmer. "I could not get anyone to take it for more. I swear to you, I have served you faithfully and well—"

"Enough. Servants. Let me see. They are not paid very well, surely."

"Well enough," said Palmer. "They only work for the length of the Season, so to speak." Palmer wondered what the duke would say if he knew exactly how very little the servants were really getting and how that very little was written down in the correct set of books, not in the doctored ones the duke was studying. For Palmer himself pocketed the difference in the servants' wages. "They have no reason to complain," he added, thinking as he did so that the servants dare not, or he would expose the shady pasts of that butler and footman and make sure that the rest of them never got another post.

"Well, I don't suppose I need to worry about the place too much," said the duke, finally closing the books. "I shall sell it as soon as the Grosvenor Square mansion is decorated. You will arrange for the servants to find new employment in my other establishments."

"Yes, your grace."

"Good. Now describe the servants at Clarges Street."

"There is a butler, John Rainbird, and a footman, Joseph. Then there is a chef, Angus MacGregor, and housekeeper, Mrs. Middleton. There are three maids. The housemaid is Alice, the chambermaid is Jenny, and there is a little scullery maid, Lizzie."

"And my arrival is expected?"

"Yes, your grace. Your grace, if I might say so, when we sell the house, I should not be putting myself out over these servants. I fear they are Jacobites and Radicals."

"Odso! Then why did you not get rid of them?"

"I only just discovered they were getting above themselves."

"You can still get rid of them in one minute."

Palmer began to sweat. His spite against the servants had landed him in a trap. Rainbird, the butler, would tell the duke the truth about the paucity of their wages if he thought he had no hope of future employment. While Rainbird had that hope, Palmer had been able to hold the threat of a bad reference over his head.

"Perhaps I was too hasty in my strictures," said Palmer hurriedly. "Your grace will no doubt decide for yourself."

"I pay you and pay you well," said the duke acidly, "so that I may not be plagued with such pettifogging questions as to whether servants have turned Jacobite or not. Now, on this one occasion, I shall deal with the matter myself. But you will present yourself before me tomorrow with the ledgers dealing with my other properties and make sure the estate agents at each place know that I shall be calling on them this year and expect to find the land in good heart and the tenants' cottages in good repair."

The duke rose to his feet, picked up his coat, and strode from the room without another look at Palmer.

Palmer groaned aloud. He had instructed the agents of each estate not to waste money on petty things such as repairs to roofs and windows. That way, he felt secure in channelling off a sizeable amount each year from each property before depositing the rest of the money in the duke's bank.

But there was still time to cover his traces. The duke had said in his letter he planned to stay in London for the rest of the Season. Then he would probably follow the Prince Regent to Brighton like the rest of the aristocrats.

It was unfortunate for the servants of Number 67 Clarges Street that the day of the duke's arrival in Town should prove to be so perfect. They had waited and waited for him to come, rooms gleaming, fresh linen on the beds, liveries and gowns brushed and pressed, their behaviour stiff and formal, their manner that of the most correct of

London servants. But as the days passed and the duke did not come, they began to become bored with waiting. That morning had dawned sunny and beautiful. The pall of smoke that usually hung over London had rolled away. A warm breeze danced along the London streets, and dust motes swam in the great shafts of sunlight that cut down through the spaces between the tall buildings.

All the windows of Number 67 were open to let in the warm, fresh air. Unknown to Palmer, the servants were nearing the end of their servitude. Season after Season, they had tucked away their tips, saving and saving, until they had now amassed enough to buy a pub. The only reason they were still servants was because of the arrival of the duke. They planned to impress the duke with their manner and behaviour, win his trust, and then tell him how little Palmer was paying them, having guessed correctly that Palmer was probably pocketing the difference between their low wages and the ones he claimed to be paying them. They knew that if they taxed the duke with this on his arrival, he would probably not believe them. A duke's agent was a very powerful man, and the duke would believe Palmer and accuse them of lying. They would never get the revenge on Palmer they craved.

Because Rainbird, the butler, and Joseph, the footman, had been dismissed in disgrace from previous employment—although innocent of the charges—Palmer had kept them bound to the house in Clarges Street with threats to ruin their characters should they try to work as servants anywhere else. The others had stayed out of loyalty to their butler and because, without a good reference, they, too, could not hope to find other work. Now, all that no longer mattered. Freedom lay ahead at the end of this very last Season.

It was Joseph who started all the trouble that beautiful day—silly, fair-haired, effeminate Joseph. He wore shoes two sizes too small for him—small feet being considered aristocratic—and the heat of the day had already begun to make his tortured feet swell. His cravat, crisply starched, jabbed into his chin. This duke would not come, grumbled Joseph to himself, and one of the most beautiful days of the year would be spent sweltering indoors.

Then there was that magnificent boat.

Angus, the Highland cook, had created a beautiful model of Nelson's flagship, the *Victory*, complete with cannon and sails. It fascinated Joseph. He wanted to see it sail and had begged the cook to let them take it to the reservoir in the Green Park, just along the road. Angus had refused, but only because this duke was about to descend on them.

There would never be another such perfect day for sailing that boat, thought Joseph pettishly. *It was folly of Rainbird to keep them kicking their heels as servants when there was no need for it.* He went moodily upstairs. Mrs. Middleton was singing in a thin, reedy voice as she arranged fresh flowers in the vases in the front parlour. Alice and Jenny were polishing and dusting rooms that surely did not need any more polishing and dusting, and Lizzie, the scullery maid who also acted as between-stairs maid, was polishing the banister with beeswax.

Rainbird was down in his pantry, sampling some claret that had arrived from the wine merchant. Angus was cooking up delicacies in the kitchen, and Dave, the pot boy—the one servant of whose existence Palmer remained unaware, Rainbird having rescued the boy from a cruel master of a chimney-sweep—was helping him.

"Lizzie!" called Joseph. Lizzie stopped polishing the banister and looked down at the footman. Joseph was an elegant and handsome creature, but the sight of him no longer made little Lizzie's heart beat any faster. On the contrary, she surveyed him with a mixture of misery and guilt, for Joseph and the others fully expected Lizzie to marry the footman as soon as their days of servitude were over, and poor Lizzie had not the courage to tell the footman she did not want to be wed to him.

"Eh wish you would not look at me lahk thet," said Joseph in his mincing and affected voice. "I h'ain't responsible for the fect we're all indoors on the bestest day this year. Lizzie, why don't you esk Rainbird to let us go to the perk and sail Angus's boat?"

"I can't," said Lizzie. "You know we're all waiting for the duke."

"We've waited and waited," said Joseph crossly. "Eh'm sick and tired of waiting."

"What's to do?" asked Rainbird, the butler, emerging from the backstairs.

"Eh want to go to the perk and sail Angus's boat," said Joseph sulkily. "This here duke ain't going to come," he added, his refined accents slipping. "We've waited every day and still he don't come. We won't get another day like this one, not for a long time."

Lizzie waited for Rainbird to curtly order the footman to go about his duties, but instead the butler looked wistfully up at the sunlight sparkling through the fanlight over the door.

"I wish we could go, Joseph," said Rainbird. "But we must impress the Duke of Pelham with our honesty, diligence, and good character, and we are not going to do that by being absent when he arrives."

"If he ever arrives," said Joseph crossly.

Rainbird stood lost in thought. He was a well-set-up

man in his forties, with an acrobat's body and a comedian's face. Even when he was sad, he seemed to be laughing at some private joke.

"We could," said the butler slowly, "always send Dave round to Palmer's office to ask if the duke is arriving today. Palmer doesn't know Dave, so he'll think he's just a messenger boy. Then, if Palmer happens to know by now the exact time of his grace's arrival—and if it's not today—then we can go."

"Huzza!" cried Joseph, capering with delight, and then letting out a shriek as his tortured feet protested.

Dave ran all the way to Holborn. Palmer studied the note from Rainbird. Then he smiled. It was obvious the duke had not gone straight to Clarges Street, and with any luck, he might catch the servants leaving. He pulled forward a sheet of paper, scribbled a note to the effect that the Duke of Pelham was not expected in London for two more days, sanded it, and handed it to Dave.

A bare two streets away, the duke browsed in the cool depths of a bookshop. He had meant to go directly to Clarges Street, but a display of all the latest books had drawn him down from his carriage.

Dave's news was greeted at 67 Clarges Street with cries of delight. Rainbird and Joseph thankfully changed out of their hot livery, Angus prepared a cold picnic lunch, and then all of them—looking for all the world like a family—set out along Clarges Street, crossed Piccadilly, and plunged into the cool shade of the Green Park.

Miss Jenny Sutherland sat in the bumping, swaying travelling carriage that was conveying her to London and hoped she would not be sick. Once Lady Letitia had made up her mind to go to Town, she had bustled about at an enormous rate. Jenny did not know that what had finally driven Lady Letitia into frenzied action was her, Jenny's, highly coloured account of what she had said to the Duke of Pelham. Lady Letitia was now afraid she had brought up a girl with neither breeding nor manners. Town bronze was what Jenny desperately needed. It was a godless age, so there was no one to advise Lady Letitia that her charge needed bronzing inside rather than out, and a lecture on humility from the vicar might have done a better job.

They were to stay with a friend of Lady Letitia's mother—"Goodness, can anyone that old be still alive?" Jenny had marvelled. Mrs. Freemantle was their London hostess's name. Lady Letitia explained that Mrs. Freemantle had never ceased from pestering her to go on a visit, and so she had sent that lady an express heralding their arrival. There was no need to waste time waiting for a reply.

Unknown to them, they nearly met the Duke of Pelham on the road. The duke had broken his journey to stay with an army friend outside London and was just setting out again on the London road as Lady Letitia's carriage bowled past. He was too preoccupied with his thoughts to notice the occupants, and Lady Letitia and Jenny were both asleep and so did not mark him either.

As Jenny already possessed a very modish wardrobe, there had been nothing to delay the ladies from setting out.

Jenny became more and more excited as London drew nearer. She thought often of the horrible Duke of Pelham. She dreamt of being an outstanding success at what was left of the Season, she dreamt of the duke falling in love with her, and her best fantasy was the one where he got down on his knees in front of her to beg her hand in marriage, and she coldly spurned him.

Her heart as yet untouched, Jenny saw marriage only

as an ambitious project. One looked for the best and the richest, and that was what one married. To be the envy of every other female in London was surely the sole goal in life. Armoured in beauty, Jenny longed to taste success, for the duke's snub still rankled.

London might seem a dirty, noisy place to some after the lush green coolness of the summer country, but as their carriage entered the busy streets, Jenny already loved everything about it: the noise, the tumult, the light carriages darting here and there like so many dragonflies skimming the choppy waters of society, the haughty ladies dressed in the bare minimum, and the strutting gentlemen with their absurdly nipped-in waists and painted faces.

"Where does Mrs. Freemantle reside?" she asked her aunt.

"Clarges Street," said Lady Letitia. "Number Seventy-one."

"And is she a pleasant lady?"

"Very. Although I have not seen her this age. Mind your manners, Jenny."

"I am always polite, Aunt Letitia."

"You have a distressing way of not listening or paying attention to anyone," said Lady Letitia sharply. "You are too wrapped up in your own appearance. There are many beautiful women in London. You will need to try to charm and please for the first time in your life. Looks are not enough on their own."

To Lady Letitia's extreme irritation, Jenny merely gave a self-satisfied little smile, as if not believing a word of it.

The carriage rumbled along Piccadilly and then was slowly reduced to a crawl in the press of traffic. The day was hot and sunny. Jenny let down the glass and leaned out.

"It all looks so carefree," she said over her shoulder

to her aunt. "Oh, look, there is a family sailing the most wonderful boat on the reservoir in the park. Are they allowed to do that? Is it not drinking water?"

"The water in London is so filthy, I do not suppose one boat will make much difference," said Lady Letitia. "That reservoir had a dead dog floating in it the last time I was in Town."

"They do seem to be enjoying themselves," said Jenny wistfully. She noticed the women of the party, with the exception of one stout older one, were in their bare feet. A tall young man had taken off his shoes and stockings and waded into the reservoir to rescue the boat, which had sailed out of reach. As she watched, he slipped and fell with an almighty splash. A park warden was hurrying towards the group, shouting in outrage. With a jerk, the carriage moved on and turned into Clarges Street, and the little tableau was lost to view.

Jenny looked down at the cool folds of her exquisitely frilled and flounced muslin gown. She had never gone barefoot or run about the fields. She did not even know what it was like to get her feet wet—outside of the bathtub, that is. She reminded herself sternly that beauties such as herself owed it to the world to protect and maintain an immaculate appearance. "Those women will probably be dreadfully sunburnt," she said, half to herself.

"We are arrived," said Lady Letitia. "Remember, now, Jenny. Best manners and best behaviour!"

"Of course," said Jenny crossly.

The carriage rolled to a stop. Lady Letitia's groom let down the carriage steps and Jenny alighted after her aunt.

What an odd-looking housekeeper! was Jenny's first thought when she saw the fantastic figure on the steps. It was that of a tall, thin woman, dressed in rusty black and with a limp muslin cap drooping over her long, horselike features. She had a great bunch of keys hanging from a chain at her waist and her muslin apron was spotted with egg stains.

"Letitia," cried this odd creature who, to Jenny's horror, ran down the steps and enfolded Lady Letitia in a warm embrace.

"Agnes, how well you look!" exclaimed Lady Letitia. "Jenny, make your curtsy. This is Mrs. Freemantle. Agnes, my niece, Jenny."

Mrs. Freemantle smiled at Jenny, baring a row of strong yellow teeth.

"Ain't you the prettiest creature that ever was!" boomed Mrs. Freemantle in a deep bass voice. "Quite like a fairy. Come in out of the heat. Tea! You must have tea."

Jenny followed her aunt and Mrs. Freemantle into the house.

The front parlour with its windows over the street was like a museum. Everything seemed to be in glass cases: stuffed animals, glass flowers, gilt clocks, figurines—all entombed in glittering glass. A vase of dusty peacock's feathers filled the cold fireplace, and lying about on a very fine Persian carpet were chunks of masonry—bases of antique pillars and headless busts. The very finding of a seat was like an obstacle race, thought Jenny, picking her way around and over objects.

How shall I ever meet any ton *people,* thought Jenny dismally, *with such a patroness?*

Lady Letitia was rattling along at a great rate about people Jenny did not know or had never heard about— mainly because she had never listened to anything Lady Letitia had said in the past that did not directly concern herself.

An elderly butler came in, bowed under the weight of a great silver tray holding teapot, hot water, milk, sugar loaves, thin bread and butter, and plum cake.

"Any gossip, Giles?" asked Mrs. Freemantle.

Giles drew himself upright, a slow creaking motion, as if he were jerking loose a series of nuts and bolts. "Yes, madam," he said. "Those strange servants from Number Sixty-seven took a boat to the park to sail it, just as if they were children. The Duke of Pelham arrived some moments ago and was in a high rage to find no one to answer the door. He has gone to his agent to get the house keys, saying loudly he meant to horse-whip every servant personally when he found them."

"Isn't Giles marvellous?" shouted Mrs. Freemantle in her loud voice. "Much better than the social columns any day. That will be all, Giles."

Jenny was shaken. Lady Letitia had picked up the thread of the conversation from where she had left off and made no mention of having met the duke, that odious pompous man. She thought with wonder of that "family" she had seen in the park. They were servants! So happy and carefree, and so soon to be whipped by that monster.

"I would like to go to my room, Mrs. Freemantle, and bathe my face," said Jenny suddenly.

"Of course, my child," shouted Mrs. Freemantle. "Come back and join us when you are freshened." She rang the bell beside her chair, an enormous brass handbell, and when Giles answered its summons, told the butler to take Miss Jenny upstairs. Jenny began to wonder if Mrs. Freemantle had any other servants.

Giles led the way up a dark narrow staircase to the second floor and creaked open a door. Jenny's bedroom was at the back. She took a shocked look around the cluttered, musty room with its great four-poster bed that hardly left room for anything else, thanked Giles faintly, and waited until he had left.

As soon as he had gone, she softly opened the door and began to creep quietly down the stairs. Why Jenny, for the first time in her selfish life, should suddenly concern herself about the welfare of others would have been a mystery to her if she had paused for thought. But she did not.

She gained the hall without meeting any servants. From behind the front parlour door came the enthusiastic roar of her hostess's voice. Quietly, she inched open the front door and let herself out into the sunny street. Casting a nervous glance over her shoulder in case she should see the monstrous Duke of Pelham watching her, Jenny ran swiftly in the direction of the Green Park—a novelty in itself, for Jenny normally moved slowly and gracefully everywhere.

The servants of Number 67 were spread about the grass at the edge of the reservoir eating a cold lunch. Jenny instinctively picked out Rainbird as the senior member, although he was not wearing livery.

"Hurry!" she cried. "Your master, the Duke of Pelham, is returned. He has gone to the agent's to get the house keys and is threatening to horse-whip all of you."

"Thank you, miss," said Rainbird. "Quickly, everyone. Move!"

Jenny had an odd longing to stay and help. But the enormity of what she had done burst over her head. She, the about-to-be toast of London, standing in the Green Park with a parcel of servants!

She picked up her skirts and ran as fast as she could back to Mrs. Freemantle's, pausing only to catch her breath outside the parlour door, before smoothing down her skirts and making a decorous entrance.

She sat quietly drinking tea, and fighting down a longing to go out on the front steps and see if she could find out what was happening.

"I tell you, Fergus," the duke was saying, as once more his carriage turned into Clarges Street, "these servants shall be sent packing! I have never heard of such insolence."

"Do not be too hasty, my lord," murmured Fergus. "There might have been some emergency."

"And what emergency," said the Duke of Pelham awfully, "could overshadow my return?"

Fergus stifled a sigh. He often felt the duke's overriding arrogance kept the kinder, pleasanter people and things of the world at bay.

Number 67 was a typical London town house of the eighteenth century. It was tall, thin, and black. Two iron dogs were chained on the steps in front, normally the only ornament in the whole of its very correct façade—except for this day.

A banner had been hung from the windows of the first floor. WELCOME HOME, YOUR GRACE, it read. The front door stood open and a trim butler in black-and-gold livery stood on the steps.

"Looks like they are expecting you after all," said Fergus.

"We shall see," said the duke. "Take the carriage down to the mews and then join me."

He strode up the steps and into the hall. Rainbird darted in front of him and held open the door of the front parlour.

Wine and cakes and biscuits lay on a polished table. There were vases of roses everywhere, their summer smell mixing comfortably with homely smells of beeswax from the furniture and sugar and vinegar from the gallipots in the corners of the room.

Rainbird bowed low and then smiled at his master. Then he snapped his fingers, and one by one the rest of the servants shuffled into the room and stood in front of the duke.

The duke looked from one face to another. The housekeeper, Mrs. Middleton, was the first to be presented. She looked frightened to death, her rabbitlike face twitching nervously under the shadow of an enormous starched linen cap. Next came Angus MacGregor, cook, his fiery hair glinting under his skull-cap, and with almost as much arrogance in his eyes as there was in those of the duke. Joseph bowed next, a great court bow with many flourishes of a scented lace handkerchief. Next came the curtsy of a housemaid of languid blond beauty—Alice. Jenny, the chambermaid, gave a quick little bob of a curtsy. Lizzie, the scullery maid, looked up at the duke with wide soft brown eyes as if pleading for mercy. The pot boy Dave bowed and tugged his forelock, and then looked around as if wishing he could hide his wizened little cockney body under one of the tables.

"Why were you not here when I first arrived?" asked the duke.

"We had been working on special preparations for your grace's arrival," said Rainbird. "Mr. Palmer informed us you were not to be expected until the day after tomorrow. We were therefore all out shopping for trifles to add to your welcome." He waved a hand that encompassed flowers and food and wine.

"In future," said the duke icily, "I expect you to be at my beck and call at all hours of the day or night. No servant is to leave the house without my express permission. Do I make myself clear?"

"Yes, your grace."

The duke's icy-blue eye fell on Lizzie's face. The little scullery maid's eyes were swimming with frightened tears.

For the first time in his life, the duke felt churlish.

The banner of welcome had startled him. He had never had a welcome before. Servants were always frightened and correct when he arrived at one of his properties and never went to any special effort beyond that of their duties.

He suddenly smiled. "I am most pleased, Rainbird, with your efforts to welcome me. I shall be dining here this evening. I now intend to change and go to my club."

"Yes, your grace."

"Now, you—Mrs. Middleton—show me to my room."

"Yes, your grace," said Mrs. Middleton, her lips trembling.

"My good woman," said the duke, but in a gentle voice, "I shall not eat you. Lead the way."

Mrs. Middleton walked before him up the stairs. "I have put your grace in here," she said, pushing open a door. "This is the largest bedroom. The dining room is next door. If your grace has guests, then there are two bedrooms prepared on the floor above."

The duke walked in and looked about. There were thick fleecy towels hanging by the toilet table, which boasted three different varieties of soap—Irish, Bristol, and Windsor. On a table beside the bed was an exquisite little flower arrangement of white roses and trailing fern. On another table in the centre of the room were spread the latest magazines, literary and sporting.

A faint smell of lavender came from the crisp white sheets turned back on the bed.

"I' faith," said the duke, "with servants such as yourself, Mrs. Middleton, a man need not search for a wife to provide a delicate and feminine touch!"

"And you must admit," said Mrs. Middleton later in the servants' hall, "no servant could ask for a higher compliment."

"Thet Palmer!" said Joseph. "He did that deliberate, you know, telling us the duke wasn't coming for another couple of days."

"Yes," agreed Rainbird. "And a right mess we'd have been in if it hadn't been for that young miss who warned us."

"Wonder who she was?" said Lizzie. "She was ever so pretty. A real lady."

"Garn!" said little Dave. "Real ladies wouldn't go to such an effort!"

"Oh yes, they would," said Rainbird. "It's the would-be ladies who don't bother about servants."

Chapter
Three

Come, and trip it, as you go,
On the light fantastic toe.

—John Milton

"Now, dear Agnes," said Lady Letitia with all the air of someone winding up a long and most satisfactory gossip, "we must nurse the ground for little Jenny so that she may have an entrée to the best houses."

"I have already been at work," shouted Mrs. Freemantle. "Clarinda Bessamy—you know, one of the Kentish Bessamys—is having a little family affair. She said that should you arrive in time, I must not stand on ceremony but bring you and your niece along. "Twill be a modest little party, but there will be cards and some dancing for the young people."

"Splendid!" said Lady Letitia. "And when is this party?"

"This very evening."

"Could not be better. Jenny has a some very fine gowns and will not appear provincial. You must go and lie down, Jenny, and rest, before your first London engagement."

Jenny left the room, trying not to look as sulky as she felt. How could she realise any of her dreams of being courted by Lord Paul and of snubbing the Duke of Pelham if she was not to move in the same circles? Mrs. Freemantle was an eccentric fright, mourned Jenny to herself as she climbed the stairs. Lady Letitia, so mondaine and elegant in the country, must really be a provincial at heart to have such a friend.

Suddenly tired after the journey, Jenny climbed into bed, quite resolved to say that evening that she had the headache and could not attend this Mrs. Bessamy's undistinguished romp.

Then she sat upright, put her hands to her white cheeks, and screamed and screamed.

Cooper, the lady's maid, came running in. Ashen-faced, Jenny pointed at the end of the bed. Seizing the poker in case it should prove to be a rat, the maid advanced cautiously on the bed, peered around the bed-hangings of the four-poster, and began to scream even louder than Jenny.

Giles came creaking in, followed by his mistress.

"Oh dear," boomed Mrs. Freemantle, "you've found them, have you? My late husband was a great traveller and I have never had the heart to throw any of his collection away. They are merely some eastern masks he brought back from his travels."

Jenny cautiously peered through her fingers. The terrible glaring faces hung at the end of her bed below the canopy proved to be nothing but grinning masks of wood and hair.

"Take them away, *please*," said Jenny.

Mrs. Freemantle instructed Giles to unhitch the masks and then followed her butler out, grumbling that she did not know where she could possibly put them now.

Lady Letitia then appeared to smooth Jenny's hair back from her brow and urge her to sleep.

"How can I possibly sleep in such a dreadful place?" complained Jenny, looking around the cluttered room. Her eye fell on an elephant's foot that held a swath of withered pampas grass, and she shuddered.

Lady Letitia slid a hand under the blankets. "The sheets have been aired, child," she said, "and the bed feels comfortable. Sleep, now, or you will not be looking your best for this evening."

After she had gone, Jenny stared up at the canopy and resolved with renewed determination not to go to this party. Then her eyes closed and she fell fast asleep.

She was awakened by the urgent cries of the lady's maid and Lady Letitia. They had forgotten to arouse her earlier, Lady Letitia explained. She must rush. Groggy with sleep, Jenny allowed herself to be bathed and dressed and curled and pomaded, and by the time she was fully awake and remembered about that headache she had meant to manufacture, it was too late.

The sight of Mrs. Freemantle in her evening finery was enough to make Jenny's heart sink right down to her little blue kid slippers.

That lady was wearing a ball dress of plain crêpe over a white satin slip of dancing length. It was trimmed round the bottom, on the sleeves, and at the waist with white velvet ribbon thickly spangled with gold. It was cut very low on the bosom, exposing an unattractive area of yellowish skin and sharp bone. She wore a fine muslin cap trimmed with priceless lace over a nut-brown wig of the cheapest variety, which looked as if it had been made from horsehair.

It was a gown designed for a daring young miss in her teens, but hardly the outfit for an old lady. Lady Letitia was wearing a dull-scarlet satin gown with a heavy necklace of antique gold. On her head was a dashing turban of pleated scarlet silk fastened with a gold-and-ruby brooch.

Jenny glanced at her own appearance in the long mirror in the hall, but the sight of her own beauty failed to raise her spirits. Her gown of delicate blue muslin with its pretty frills and tucks over a chemisette of white embroidered lawn had never been worn before. She remembered crossly how many dreams she had woven about this gown and how she had been saving it for a very special occasion.

Now it would be exposed to the vulgar stare of a bunch of Nobodies!

At that moment, the Duke of Pelham was critically surveying his own appearance in the glass at Number 67 Clarges Street. He was wearing an evening coat of dull-green silk with gold buttons over a waistcoat of green-and-gold-striped marseilles. His cravat was tied in the Mathematical. His breeches of double-milled stocking were stretched over his powerful thighs like a second skin and tied at the knee with gold ribbons—sixteen "strings," as they were called, to each knee. He hung his dress sword at his side and tucked his bicorne under his arm.

"Have you my bits and pieces?" he said over his shoulder to Fergus.

"Yes, your grace. I have your scent bottle and fan, card money, and two clean handkerchiefs."

"Good. We are set. I wish I had not said I would go. But I let Mannering coerce me into it."

The duke shook his head as he thought of the events

of the day. He had refused all leave from the wars until now, feeling it his duty to fight for his country for as long as he was able. But a severe bout of fever had landed him in hospital, and he had been urged to take his long-overdue leave. Feeling weak and sick and helpless, he had taken a ship at Portugal, only to find that all the benefits of sun and fresh air on a good journey home had completely restored him to health. But he was homesick and anxious to see England again. He also felt it was high time he found a wife and started his nursery. He had forgotten the extravagance of dress and the oddity of manners of London society, which now struck him as weird and wonderful.

He had even forgotten the fashion for weeping copiously on all occasions. A gentleman was expected to have "bottom"—meaning courage, coolness, and solidity. But a gentleman was also expected to have sensibility. It was an age in which the diarist Thomas Creevey coined the phrase "not a dry eye in the house," by which he meant the House of Commons, where politicians would vie with each other to see who could cry the most.

The jealousy of accomplished weepers was not confined to the men. Even that brilliant and frivolous novelist, Fanny Burney, herself an accomplished weeper, could not bear to be beaten and became quite cattish over a certain Sophy Streatfield, who seemed to be able to weep at will.

An elderly lord had dropped dead in White's a bare half hour before the duke's arrival there earlier in the day, and all the members were roaring and bawling and crying as if he had been their dearest, closest relative, instead of a crusty old gentleman of loose morals who had risen to meet his Maker in a cloud of brandy fumes.

So the duke, accustomed to the stern faces and stoic courage of the battlefield, was quite appalled, and therefore relieved, to find the one dry-eyed member of the club, Lord Paul Mannering, seated in the coffee room.

Lord Paul, like the duke, had just come to Town, but said he had encountered Mrs. Bessamy in Pall Mall, and that lady had urged him to attend her little party and to bring Pelham along as well.

"How does she know of me?" the duke had asked.

"Because I told her I met you on the road to London," explained Lord Paul. "Do say you will come. London seems a devilish strange place to me, all primping men and half-naked women."

It had seemed like a good idea to the duke, and he had asked Rainbird for his dinner to be set before him at six o'clock.

But that dinner had proved to be the most exquisite he had ever tasted. The house was clean and smelled sweet. The servants moved efficiently and unobtrusively about their duties. The ghost of his dead father did not rise to plague him. For the first time in his life, he had an odd feeling of being at home. He felt he should question that Rainbird fellow about his Radical views, but somehow could not bring himself to spoil the family atmosphere. Yes, that's what is was! It was not like being the master of a house full of strange servants, but of being a well-loved relative arriving home at last. Odd. He wished with all his heart he had not agreed to go out.

"Quarters all right, Fergus?" he finally remembered to ask his servant.

"Yes, very comfortable, your grace."

"Are the other servants courteous to you and mindful of your rank as my personal servant?"

Fergus turned away to hide a grin. It was his opinion that that odd bunch downstairs were, underneath, not particularly mindful of any rank. And then there was Alice. Sweet, beautiful, golden Alice, the housemaid, whose voice as soft as Cornish cream fell easily on his ears. Anxious all of a sudden to see himself through Alice's eyes, Fergus peered over his master's shoulder and looked in the glass. He was dressed in his new livery of pale blue velvet with silver lacing. He was thirty-five, but he noticed that the silvering of his hair at the temples made him appear older. A little judicious application of dye might perhaps help, he thought, turning his head from side to side. His face was too brown; the wars had carved deep lines on either side of his mouth, and his brown eyes had a wary look. But he had a good figure, a straight nose, and a firm mouth. His legs did not require false calves or padding. His . . .

"Do tell me if I am blocking your view," said the duke acidly.

"No, your grace," said Fergus, falling back a pace. "I was only checking to make sure I did you justice."

"When did you ever trouble about your appearance before, my Fergus?" The duke laughed. "Which one is it? The inestimable housekeeper with the large cap?"

"She is too old for me," said Fergus sharply. The duke gave his servant an amused smile and turned to leave.

Feeling thoroughly depressed, Fergus followed his master from the room.

Still sulky, Jenny Sutherland picked up her filmy skirts and followed her aunt and hostess into the carriage. She prepared herself for a long journey to some undistinguished part of town. Bloomsbury, perhaps. Oh, horrors!

She was amazed to find they had gone only a short distance when the carriage rolled to a halt. Wondering, Jenny stepped down onto the pavement. She was facing a great town house with lights blazing from every window. A line of powdered footmen with stiffened gold-embroidered skirts to their coats and wearing gold swords lined the steps on either side of the entrance.

"Gracious!" said Jenny. "Is this Mrs. Bessamy's?"

"Of course, my love," said Lady Letitia, flashing a cynical look at her niece. "What did you expect? Mrs. Bessamy is very good *ton.*"

"But she does not have a title?"

"Shhh! Do not betray your lack of sophistication to Mrs. Freemantle. Often the untitled members of society hold more sway that the titled. After all, Brummell is plain 'mister.'"

In a daze, Jenny followed her chaperones up a curved staircase to a chain of saloons on the first floor. Mrs. Bessamy was a small, fussy blonde woman, plump and undistinguished in appearance, but covered from head to foot in jewels that looked as if they had been thrown at her by her dresser, rather like throwing darts. She even had diamond brooches pinned randomly over the skirts of her gown. She wore a great, heavy tiara, a mixture of diamonds, rubies, and several semi-precious stones. Her fat face under it was small and creased with parallel wrinkles, so that it looked as if it might spring back into its normal shape once the weight of the great tiara was removed.

Mrs. Freemantle was welcomed warmly. Jenny was introduced to a bewildering selection of people. Powder was often still worn in the country, but most gentlemen wore their own hair. A combination of the iniquitous flour tax and the fact that Wellington had stopped the army from buying sixty-five hundred tons of flour a year for powdering had made a difference. Some regretted its passing and longed for what they considered the more elegant days

43

when the Prince de Kaunitz, who wore satin stays, would pass a portion of every morning walking up and down a room in which four valets puffed a cloud of scented powder at his head, each of a different colour, in order that it might fall and amalgamate into the exact nuance that best suited their master's taste.

Jenny had lost much of her usual poise. It was an odd world where such freaks as Mrs. Bessamy and Mrs. Freemantle were hailed with affection, and yet titled and beautiful ladies were not rated nearly so high.

The London voices of the *ton* were different from what Jenny had expected, and so she listened hard so as to try to copy this strange accent. Spoil, for example, was pronounced "spile," Lord Byron as "Lord Birron," London as "Lonnon." "Contemplate" and "balcony" had the emphasis on the first syllable, which was very odd to Jenny, who had, hithertofore, heard the gentry speak only of balcoNIES and of conTEMPlating something or other. Tea was still pronounced "tay." At least no one had tried to change that, and probably never would, thought Jenny.

She walked sedately through the saloons between Lady Letitia and Mrs. Freemantle and kept her eyes and ears open. She had never before been in rooms so brightly lit or so opulently furnished, so decorated with flowers and swathes of silk. In one of the main saloons was a little marble fountain spouting champagne instead of water. "Quite silly, really," boomed Mrs. Freemantle. "Takes out all the fizz. Would you like some, Jenny?"

"Thank you, Mrs. Freemantle," said Jenny politely. "I am most obleeged."

"No, no, no," said Mrs. Freemantle in a stage whisper that nonetheless carried from end to end of the rooms. "You must not say 'obleeged.' Obliged, my girl. Obliged."

"But the Prince Regent himself is reported to say 'obleeged,' " said Jenny crossly.

"Not by the time his elocution teacher, John Kemble, has finished with him, he won't," said Mrs. Freemantle, slapping her hip with her fan and roaring with laughter. "Why, only t'other day, Kemble said, 'Sir, may I beseech your Royal Highness to open your royal jaws and say 'oblige'?'

Mrs. Bessamy came hurrying up. "Prinny will be here shortly, Mrs. Freemantle. Was there ever such a pest of a man? He was not invited, you know."

Jenny stood round-eyed with wonder. The Prince Regent himself was to attend, and yet this hostess was not pleased!

Then she saw Lord Paul Mannering walking towards them, forgot she hardly knew him, and called to him, quite boldly, "Do but come and see this pretty fountain, my lord."

"Jenny," hissed Lady Letitia, quite distressed.

But Lord Paul came up to them, smiled at Jenny, and bowed low before Lady Letitia. "I believe there is to be dancing," he said. "May I hope you will do me the honour . . ."

"Of course, my lord," said Jenny, all dimples and smiles, and then wondered what there was about her acceptance of his invitation to make him look so startled and make her aunt frown.

Lord Paul looked away from Jenny as if embarrassed, and then his face lit up. "Here is Pelham," he cried. "I am so glad he decided to come."

The duke smiled a welcome to Lord Paul, bowed to Lady Letitia and Mrs. Freemantle, and ignored Jenny, who blushed furiously.

A stentorian voice from the doorway announced the arrival of the Prince Regent. The guests shuffled into two lines.

The prince was a corpulent man, and his blue eyes held the watery glitter of the habitual drinker. " 'Tis a mercy he only likes ladies old enough to be his grandmother," Jenny heard Lady Letitia mutter. "My Jenny will be safe enough."

"Your niece is so beautiful," whispered Lord Paul, "that I doubt if she will be safe from anyone this evening, even Prinny."

Jenny's eyes shone like stars at the compliment. She straightened her spine and when the Prince Regent approached her, she sank into a graceful curtsy.

"Hey, who have we here?" cried the prince.

"Miss Jenny Sutherland," said Mrs. Bessamy. "One of our newest débutantes."

It was true the Prince Regent did not usually bother with young misses, but there was something about Jenny's fresh beauty and the blue of her gown that touched a sentimental chord in his fat royal heart.

"I shall take pretty Miss Sutherland to waltz," said the prince with great good humour. "Music, hey!"

The orchestra at the end of the room struck up, and the guests moved to the side of the floor as the prince put his arm around Jenny's waist to lead her in the steps of the dance. "You must do exactly what his Royal Highness does," she heard her aunt whisper desperately.

It did not take Jenny long to realise her royal partner was very drunk. He reeled and staggered, and to her mortification, he forced her to reel and stagger as well. She looked desperately to her aunt for guidance and received a quick nod to indicate she was doing just as she ought. If the Prince Regent danced drunkenly, then any lady dancing with him must appear to be drunk as well. Such was the peculiar etiquette. It was dreadful to hear the titters as they staggered and swayed and stumbled.

After this had been going on for an agonising ten minutes, the prince became bored, stopped and turned away, and called, "Bring my toy, and let us see how the ladies perform."

An aide carried in an air gun, which he presented to the prince. The prince strode through the rooms until he came to a smaller one. He ordered playing cards to be put up on the end wall, and then took aim. He had a remarkable eye for one so drunk. Then he called to the ladies to try their aim. Mrs. Bessamy was heard to groan. Lady Letitia said loudly that she was very short-sighted, and many of the other ladies followed her lead. Several did try, but the shooting match was soon called to a halt, not because someone had shot one of the fiddlers in the orchestra—for who cared about a mere fiddler?—but because a giggling miss had succeeded in putting a dart into the painted eye of one of Mrs. Bessamy's ancestors whose portrait hung some way away from the targets.

The prince said sulkily he would play cards and went off with his cronies. Dancing commenced in the main room.

Jenny found herself standing beside Lord Paul and Lady Letitia. She smiled up hopefully at Lord Paul. It was again the inevitable waltz, and he had voiced a desire to dance with her.

The Duke of Pelham joined them. He was a most unpleasant and unsettling man, thought Jenny. He looked over her head as if she did not exist and said to Lady Letitia, "Would you care to dance with me, ma'am?"

Lord Paul muttered something under his breath. Lady Letitia appeared a little startled, but she nodded and curtsied and allowed him to lead her onto the floor. Lord Paul must really dislike the duke as well, thought Jenny, seeing her companion glower after the couple.

"He is really a dreadfully overbearing man," commented Jenny.

"Who?" demanded Lord Paul crossly, his eyes still on the duke and Lady Letitia.

"Why, the Duke of Pelham, of course."

Lord Paul looked down at Jenny. "You cannot know, Miss Sutherland, that I admire Pelham greatly as a soldier and a gentleman, or you would not have made such an odd remark. Excuse me." He bowed and walked across the room to where a vivacious little girl with a face like a pug was standing, and the next thing Jenny knew, Lord Paul was leading pug-face onto the floor, looking delighted with his company.

Jenny sat down on a little gilt chair and fanned herself. She felt lost and bewildered. There was no other woman in the room as beautiful as Jenny Sutherland, and yet it appeared she was to be a wallflower.

She sat through that dance and then sat through another. She had the mortification of seeing Lady Letitia anxiously making her way to join her niece, only to be asked to dance with Lord Paul. The Duke of Pelham led pug-face onto the floor and seemed as delighted with her as Lord Paul had been.

Dancers danced, society members strolled past, their hard, assessing eyes resting indifferently on Jenny and then looking away.

It was too much to bear. Jenny rose to her feet and hurried away to try to find a quiet corner to hide her humiliation.

At the end of the chain of saloons was a closed door.

She pushed it open and found herself in a little library. She closed the door behind her, shutting off the chatter and music.

She sat down and opened and shut her fan while she tried to sort out her thoughts. Why was she not a success? What if someone from her home town should come to London, someone like Euphemia Vickers, who would return after her visit to tell everyone how their belle had been spurned?

What was there about that pug-faced little girl in the undistinguished dress that drew such people as the duke and Lord Paul to her side?

"It must be the fault of Mrs. Bessamy," decided Jenny at last with all the hypersensitivity of the young. "She is jealous of me, and has put about bad things about me to ruin my social career." And the more she thought about it, the more Jenny decided that this must be the case. Mrs. Bessamy's uninterested gaze began, in retrospect, to hold a world of malice and envy.

There are wicked people in London, mused Jenny, beginning to feel comforted. *But I shall wait a little and then tell Aunt I must go home.*

She saw some magazines lying on a table in front of her, picked up one, opened it at the beginning of a serial, and began to read.

She became so engrossed in the story that she forgot the passing of time until the sound of the turning of the handle of the library door made her start.

Without thinking, she dropped the magazine, darted behind her chair and crouched down.

"There appears to be nobody here" came Lord Paul's voice.

Then came the voice of Lady Letitia, sharp and worried. "Where can that child have gone to?"

"Not very far, I think," replied Lord Paul. "Mrs. Bessamy always promises little family parties and they always turn into a sad crush."

"I am taking you away from your partners, my lord," said Lady Letitia.

"Not quite," said Lord Paul. "But I crave a dance now with the most attractive lady in the room."

"Oh, *Jenny,*" said Lady Letitia with a little laugh. "Yes, as usual, she is the most beautiful creature here. It puzzles me why she has not taken. I must search further. Perhaps, my lord, if we separate and search on different sides of the room."

"Gladly. Good, here is Pelham. He shall assist us."

"I shall start my search immediately, my lord," said Lady Letitia. "I confess to becoming monstrous worried."

Her last words were fainter as she moved away.

Then to Jenny's listening ears came the Duke of Pelham's voice. "What troubles Lady Letitia?"

"Miss Jenny Sutherland is nowhere to be found."

"She is probably hiding somewhere. Having failed to get any attention by fair means, she has no doubt resorted to foul. By that, I mean she is probably hiding behind some curtain waiting until her disappearance has created enough of a fuss."

Jenny stifled a gasp of outrage.

"You are too hard" came Lord Paul's voice. "Help me search. After I have found her, I think I shall go home. I am tired after the journey."

"I shall probably stay until dawn at least," said the Duke of Pelham. "Little Miss Maddox is delightful company."

Pug-face, no doubt, thought Jenny.

"It is a wonder the beautiful Miss Jenny was not besieged with admirers," said Lord Paul.

"That is easy to explain," said the duke. "Confess! You know the reason as well as I."

But Lord Paul's reply was drowned in the sound of the closing of the door as both men went out of the room.

Jenny slowly straightened up and went to the mirror and looked at her own glowing reflection. What had gone wrong? Why was her failure so marked it was being discussed by Lord Paul and the loathsome duke?

The headache she had been planning to fake all day suddenly became a reality. She slipped from the room and went in search of her aunt.

"So I became bored," said Jenny in the carriage home, "and wanted a little time to myself. That is why I disappeared, Aunt, so do not keep asking and asking."

"Jenny," said Lady Letitia, "your country manners will not answer in London. There is a boldness about your air and mien, an expectation of attracting all eyes to you, which I fear makes the gentlemen decide to ignore you. You are an unknown. The favourites among the new débutantes are already well established. You would do well to copy the air and attitude of Miss Maddox."

"Who is she?"

"The attractive brunette who danced first with Lord Paul."

"But she has nothing in the way of looks. She looks like a pug-dog with her little squashed-up face!"

"Jenny! When will you ever learn that . . . oh! You infuriating girl, you are not paying the slightest heed to a single word I am saying!"

And Jenny was not. For as the carriage slowed and they approached Mrs. Freemantle's, Jenny looked down from the carriage window and caught a glimpse of the servants of Number 67, sitting around a table in their servants' hall. It was an odd view, seen as it was through the high-up window, revealing Joseph playing the mandolin and the tops of the heads of the rest as they sang to its accompaniment.

Lady Letitia and Jenny climbed down. Lady Letitia sent the carriage back to wait for Mrs. Freemantle, that energetic old lady having vowed to stay all night.

"At least Lord Paul seems quite taken with me," said Jenny defiantly as they mounted the stairs.

"And what on earth gave you that idea?" said Lady Letitia, becoming very angry indeed.

But Jenny could not reveal she had been listening in the library when she heard Lord Paul describe her, as she thought, as the most attractive lady in the room.

"And he is much too old for you," went on Lady Letitia, seeing Jenny did not reply.

"Pooh! He is very handsome. And let me tell you this, I am quite convinced Mrs. Bessamy said something spiteful about me to make me unpopular."

"Go to bed, Jenny," said Lady Letitia, and Jenny looked in surprise at her normally tranquil aunt's furious face revealed in the light of the oil-lamp she was carrying. "You weary me with your vanity and stupidity and want of courtesy, manners, or generosity of heart! Mrs. Bessamy is all that is kind. She told me she was worried over your wallflower status and did her best to alleviate it, but not one gentleman could be persuaded to take you to the floor."

Lady Letitia went into her room and slammed the door in Jenny's face.

Jenny ran into her own room, threw herself down on the bed and cried and cried. What had gone wrong? Aunt Letitia had always been kind and warm and loving. What had made her say all those terrible things, none of which could possibly be true? "I am *not* selfish," said Jenny at last, sitting up and scrubbing her eyes with a handkerchief. "If it had not been for me, those servants of Pelham's would have been in dire trouble."

Cooper came in to prepare Jenny for bed, but Jenny told the maid to go away.

The beginnings of a mad idea were beginning to take shape in her brain. She craved admiration as another might crave a drug. For Jenny, her own beauty really existed only in her reflection seen in other people's eyes. Those servants of Pelham had every reason to be grateful to her. Why, she must be a heroine in their eyes! Pelham had said he would stay all night. She would let herself out of Mrs. Freemantle's, as she had done earlier, and slip along to Number 67 and surprise them. How delighted they would be to see her! How admiring! How respectful!

Jenny bathed her red eyes in cold water and tucked several stray curls back into place. The night was very warm, and she would not need a pelisse or a shawl.

Having made up her mind, she no longer hesitated to consider the folly of what she was doing.

She let herself quietly out of the house and took a deep breath of warm, gritty night-time London air before darting along the street and down the area steps of Number 67.

"Stop playing, Joseph!" called Rainbird. "There's someone at the door."

"Whoever could it be at this time of night?" exclaimed Mrs. Middleton. "You had best take Angus here with you in case it prove to be villains."

"I don't think villains would knock loudly for entrance," said the butler, looking at Angus with amusement as the cook unhooked a great blunderbuss from the wall.

He opened the door. Angus poked the muzzle of the blunderbuss over Rainbird's shoulder. Jenny Sutherland stood on the doorstep.

"Why, miss!" said Rainbird, backing a pace in surprise and bumping into Angus. "Whatever is the matter?"

"I had to speak to you," said Jenny. "Let me in."

"But your parents . . ."

"Both dead. Let me in."

Rainbird stood his ground. "You must have some sort of relative or chaperone."

"I am Miss Jenny Sutherland," said Jenny. "My aunt is in bed. No one will miss me. I reside at Number Seventy-one. I only want to talk for a little. I thought you would be glad to see me."

"Very well," said Rainbird. He and Angus stood aside, and Jenny, still in her ball-gown, tripped into the servants' hall. The rest rose and stood at attention.

"Please sit down, Miss Sutherland," said Rainbird, pulling out a chair for her. "Miss Sutherland," he said to the rest, "is the young lady who warned us of the Duke of Pelham's return."

"Yes, but what is Miss Sutherland doing here at this hour of the night?" demanded Mrs. Middleton, her face twitching nervously as she imagined wrathful parents or guardians erupting into the servants' hall.

"Miss Sutherland is about to explain that," said Rainbird. He poured Jenny a glass of wine, sat down beside her, and indicated to the others that they might be seated as well.

"Now, Miss Sutherland," said Rainbird, "please explain how we can be of assistance to you."

Jenny looked about the candle-lit group. Joseph was holding a beribboned mandolin on his knee and gazing at her in open admiration. Mrs. Middleton was looking as stern and disapproving as that kindly lady could manage to look. Lizzie's large, pansy-brown eyes were fastened on Jenny's face like those of a child waiting for a bedtime story. Alice was hemming a handkerchief. She raised her head and smiled at Jenny, a warm, encouraging smile.

Jenny drank a little of her wine and remained silent.

"I shall introduce myself and then the others while you compose yourself," said Rainbird. "I am Rainbird, butler. The distinguished lady with the cap is Mrs. Middleton. The fiery Scotchman in the skull-cap is Angus MacGregor. Our brunette has the same name as yours, Jenny, the chambermaid. Alice is the housemaid, the one with the sewing. Joseph, the footman, has been entertaining us on the mandolin. Lizzie is our"—he hesitated. He had been about to say "scullery maid," but Lizzie had changed so much, had grown in mind and stature, and soon they were to have their freedom and Lizzie would be their equal. "Lizzie is our general maid," he said, and Lizzie went quite pink with delight at the grand new title. "And little Dave is our pot boy."

Jenny smiled tremulously.

"Now, you cannot stay long," said Rainbird. "Do please tell us what troubles you. I assure you none of us will gossip." Rainbird flashed a warning at Joseph, that arch-gossip, and then turned back to Jenny. She looked at the butler's clever, funny face, at his sparkling grey eyes, and gave a little laugh.

"I went to my first London party this evening," said

Jenny, "and no one would dance with me, although I was by far the prettiest lady there. I was a failure. There was a girl with a face like a pug-dog and everyone seemed to love her, and Aunt Letitia says I am. . . . v-vain . . . and . . . and . . .s-selfish . . ." And with that, Jenny buried her face in her hands and began to cry again.

She made a pathetic figure. Angus cleared his throat and turned away, Mrs. Middleton brushed sympathetic tears from her own eyes, and Dave gave something like a sniff, wiped his nose defiantly on his sleeve, and glared about the group.

Rainbird handed Jenny a large clean handkerchief. He waited patiently until she had hiccupped and sobbed her way into silence and then said quietly, "Did you say you were the prettiest lady there?"

"Y-yes," said Jenny, giving her nose a hard blow.

"And what gave you that idea, miss?" asked Rainbird.

Jenny looked at him in amazement. "But one has only to look at me!" she said.

"But looks are nothing compared to warmth and animation," cried Rainbird. "No one is beautiful outside if they are not beautiful inside."

"Well!" breathed Jenny. "And after all I did for you, you dare to insult me . . . you, a servant!"

"You came for help," said Rainbird calmly. "It appears to me you have relied solely on your beauty and nothing else, and so the development of your character has been stunted. It is very unbecoming in a lady to voice openly that she thinks she is prettier than anyone else. Now, the pug-faced lady may have been full of laughter and warmth and fun."

"Yes, she was," said Jenny bitterly, "as well she might be with all the gentlemen vying for her attentions."

"But not vain. Not proud."

Jenny hung her head.

"No," she whispered.

"Well, there you are," said Rainbird cheerfully. "The next function you attend, you must put thoughts of your own appearance outside your mind. You must appear to be as delighted with unimportant men who dance with you as important. You must, should you find yourself a wallflower, seek the company of another wallflower and try to cheer and comfort her. You must not look in the glass for a month."

Despite her shame and misery, Jenny gave a reluctant laugh. "But how can I arrange my hair?"

"Your maid arranges it. You shut your eyes and think of something else." He shut his own eyes and went through a comical mime of a lady trying to ignore her appearance, opening his eyes and appearing to stare rapturously at his own expression, and then shutting them firmly and sitting there with a pious look on his face.

With the mercurial change of spirits that bless the young, Jenny began to feel as ridiculously light-hearted as she had been miserable before.

"And," said Rainbird, "seek out Miss Pug-Face and instead of envying her—"

"I! Envy her?"

"Yes, instead of envying her, try to copy her manner."

"Why should I take your advice?" demanded Jenny. "It is not as if you go about in society."

"Oh, but I do," said Rainbird, "if only in my capacity as servant." And he added with deliberate rudeness, "And any one of us here has better social manners than you any day, my hoity-toity miss."

Jenny bristled like an angry kitten. But Alice continued

to sew, and the rest continued to look at her with open sympathy, as if they were her equals and not servants at all.

"I came here for comfort and all I get is a jaw-me-dead," said Jenny.

"Jaw-me-deads can be very comforting in retrospect," said Rainbird seriously. "You can try it my way for a little and then, if it does not work, why, you can come and lecture me on the vanity of trying to arrange someone else's life."

"What an odd lot of people you are," said Jenny. "Are you related to each other?"

"Only by the chains of servitude," said Rainbird solemnly. To Jenny's amazement, he got to his feet and cartwheeled around the table, to land neatly back in his chair.

"Mr. Rainbird used to perform at the fairs," said Dave, clapping with glee. "Do it again, Mr. Rainbird."

"No," said the butler. "I want wine and music."

"I have been listening to music all evening and longing to dance," said Jenny wistfully, "but no one asked me."

"Play, Joseph!" cried Rainbird. He jumped to his feet and bowed low before Jenny. "Would Miss Sutherland do me the inestimable honour of allowing me to lead her to the floor?"

There were cheers and claps, and to Jenny's bewilderment, the servants rose and pushed the table back against the wall. Joseph struck a jaunty chord.

"Why not?" laughed Jenny, taking Rainbird's hand.

They formed a set for a country dance, Rainbird at the top with Jenny, Mrs. Middleton with Angus, Alice and chambermaid-Jenny, and Lizzie and Dave.

Just then the Duke of Pelham climbed down from his carriage and listened in amazement to the sounds of merriment coming from his servants' hall.

"Probably getting drunk on my wine," he said furiously to Fergus.

He was in a bad mood, caused, had he but realised it, by his own uneasy conscience. For he had been largely responsible for Jenny's social failure. It had made him furious to see her standing there as if expecting homage from everyone who set eyes on her. Not quite realising that a handsome and rich duke newly returned from the wars had almost absolute social power, he had commented acidly to one young man who had appeared smitten with Jenny's looks, "Miss Sutherland is a country nobody with neither charm nor wit. Not the partner for a gentleman of fashion." To his irritation, the young man had immediately joined a large group of other gentlemen to relay this piece of gossip. He saw the insolent, contemptuous stares cast in Jenny's direction but refused to admit to himself he was responsible for her humiliation. But when Jenny had left and he no longer had the doubtful joy of seeing the mortification of Miss Jenny Sutherland, who had dared to be rude to him at a country ball, the evening had gone sadly flat.

He marched into his front parlour and stretched his hand out towards the bell. No! He would confront these servants. "Stay here, Fergus," he commanded, seeing his servant sliding in the direction of the door. "I will deal with this myself."

He walked down the backstairs and threw open the door of the servants' hall. Miss Jenny Sutherland was twirling around in the arms of his butler while the other servants laughed and cheered.

She was the first to see him. She let out a gasp of horror, all happiness and life draining from her face.

"What is the meaning of this?" demanded the Duke of Pelham.

Jenny half-turned to flee, to leave these odd servants to face the wrath of their master, but something made her stand her ground.

"The fault is mine, your grace," she said defiantly. "I had a miserable time this evening. I saw your servants from the carriage window and they looked so comfortable, so happy, and so at ease, that I decided to call on them. We do such things in the country," said Jenny airily, although she knew it would be as shocking in the country for a lady to visit servants in the middle of the night as it was in Town. "I was unhappy because I had been unable to dance at the party. I commanded Mr. Rainbird to dance with me. Your servants were obliged to obey that command."

The duke's frigid stare raked round the room. The servants looked back calmly, and quite unafraid. Even Mrs. Middleton wasn't twitching, he noticed. He did not know that each servant had just reminded him- or herself that liberty was just around the corner, and, the trouncing of Palmer apart, they had nothing to fear from the dislike of the Duke of Pelham.

"Your aunt shall hear of this, Miss Sutherland," said the duke.

"Think of your aunt, don't think of your looks," came a voice at her ear, but Jenny wondered afterwards whether that voice had been Rainbird's or a voice in her own head.

"Your grace," said Jenny, "my aunt has done everything for me; she has brought me up and looked after me like a daughter. By telling her, you would not be punishing me, but Lady Letitia. I beg your mercy."

The duke looked down at the defiant little figure. Several of her curls had come loose from her headdress and were hanging in disarray about her shoulders. "I shall not tell Lady Letitia," he heard himself say. "But my servants should not have encouraged you in this folly and must be punished."

"Ah, no!" said Jenny. "They were only being kind! See how red my eyes are with weeping? They were only trying to comfort me."

The duke swung round and stared at the wall. He had not thought Miss Sutherland had any feelings at all. She was little more than a child, and he had made her cry by ruining her social standing.

He swung back and faced them. "Perhaps it would be better if we forgot about the whole sorry affair. Do not disgrace yourself thus again, Miss Jenny, if you have any care for your aunt."

For that one moment, Jenny found herself liking him enormously.

"Then you must dance with me, your grace, before I go home."

"No, no, no," whispered Rainbird. "You have gone too far."

But the duke smiled, that enchanting smile of his, and said, "Of course."

Fergus, dreading the glorious Alice was being dismissed by his wrathful master, crept to the door of the servants' hall and listened in amazement to the continued sounds of merriment coming from within. He cautiously pushed open the door.

The duke was waltzing with none other than that young miss who had been at the country ball and whom he had seen only just that evening leaving Mrs. Bessamy's while he stood with the other servants in the hall.

"Come and join us, Fergus," cried the duke.

Fergus promptly hurried into the room and claimed Alice's hand for a dance.

Jenny looked up in a bewildered way at the duke, wondering whether he might have a heart after all. He smiled at her and she bent her head in confusion and her dark curls tickled his chin. She was nothing more than a wilful child, thought the duke indulgently. He would repair the harm he had done her reputation at the first opportunity.

The music ceased. The duke still stood, his hand at Jenny's waist, looking down at her. Jenny felt hot and confused, a mixture of bewildering emotions surging through her.

"I must go now," she said, pulling away.

"Then I shall accompany you," said the duke.

"No!" said Jenny. "If I am spotted I can say I fell asleep with my clothes on and have been sleep-walking." She turned and ran out of the door, up the area steps, and soon the diminishing patter of her feet could be heard coming from the pavement above.

Chapter
Four

Me this unchartered freedom tires;
I feel the weight of chance desires;

—William Wordsworth

Mrs. Freemantle made a noisy return as a red dawn rose over London. She was considered an Original and had been escorted back to Clarges Street by a party of noisy young bucks. She kissed them all good night and then lurched unsteadily into the front parlour.

Lady Letitia, roused from an uneasy sleep by all the noises outside, pulled on her wrapper and made her way downstairs.

Mrs. Freemantle was slumped in a chair by the hearth when Lady Letitia entered the room. She exuded a strong smell of spirits. Her cap lay in a crumpled heap at her feet and her wig had slipped over one eye. She had her eyes closed.

Lady Letitia shook her gently by the shoulder. "Agnes," she said, "you must not fall asleep here."

"Hey, what!" Mrs. Freemantle opened her eyes and

looked about her in a dazed way, and then up into Lady Letitia's anxious face. "Oh, Letisha," she slurred. "Jolly, jolly party. Pelham left 'fore I could shlap his shtupid face with my fan."

"Why should you want to do that?"

"What he did to Jenny." Mrs. Freemantle's eyes began to close.

"Now, this is something I must learn," muttered Lady Letitia. She made her way down to the kitchen and brewed a pot of strong black coffee. She was of the old school who considered only upstarts roused their servants during the night to perform trivial tasks—although it was rumoured that the Prince Regent rang for his valet about forty times a night, demanding to know the time, even though he had a watch beside his bed.

She carried cups and coffee upstairs, roused Mrs. Freemantle again, and demanded she drink at least two cups. "For I must know what you meant by that remark about Pelham."

Mrs. Freemantle groggily did as she was bid and then sat up looking bright and sober. It was a hard-drinking age, and Lady Letitia knew from experience that her friend's sobriety would be only temporary.

"Now, Agnes," she urged, "tell me about Pelham and Jenny."

"Infuriating man," roared Mrs. Freemantle, pouring another cup of coffee and draining it in one gulp. "He ups and damns Miss Jenny as having neither wit nor charm. He says something about no gentleman of fashion should be seen dead dancing with her and quite ruined her."

"Oh dear," said Lady Letitia, "what shall I do? I confess I berated poor Jenny and told her that her lack of success was entirely due to her own vanity."

"Do not exercise yourself too much," said Mrs. Freemantle, her old eyes suddenly sharp and shrewd. "It was montrous of Pelham, and I repaired much of the damage before the evening was out, but Jenny needs a set-down. I could not help noticing the contemptuous glances that young lady cast on me. She sets too much store on the outsides of people. How did it come about? You had the raising of her, Letitia."

"I am afraid I left her for too many years in the charge of an undemanding governess," said Lady Letitia ruefully. "I did at times feel she should be taught something more academic than Italian, water-colouring, and playing the pianoforte. But no one wants an intelligent girl. She has always been charming and beautiful and pleasing to people. She finished with her governess a short time ago, and it was only then I realised how vain she had become."

"As long as she learns to appear modest," said Mrs. Freemantle, "then that is all that is required. You will soon be shot of her. With looks like hers, she will have her pick."

"But I love Jenny, and want her to be happy, and vain people are never happy."

"Fustian. London's full of coxcombs who start their day each morning by admiring themselves in the glass. They are so pleased with themselves they never notice anyone else. It is quite the fashion . . . vanity, I mean. But don't tell the child about Pelham. It will do her no harm to think she brought about her humiliation all by herself . . . that is, if you mean to reform her character. Now, we go to the Denbys' musicale tonight. She will have a chance to shine."

"Do you always rattle about London at such a rate?" asked Lady Letitia.

"Always," said Mrs. Freemantle, with a cavernous yawn. "Keeps me alive."

The brief party at Number 67 was over a few minutes after Jenny had left. Fergus prepared his master for bed and returned to the servants' hall. They were all seated around the table again, studying a newspaper cutting, which was tucked out of sight into Rainbird's pocket as soon as he appeared. Fergus tried to make conversation, but they so obviously wanted to be rid of him that he took himself, rather sadly, off to bed.

"Now," said Rainbird, producing the cutting again, "there is this pub for sale in Highgate. It has stood empty for some time, so we will get it cheaply. It must need a lot of work, for it stands on the main road north. But we shall contrive, and a low price will leave us plenty to engage carpenters and builders. As soon as his grace takes himself off tomorrow—I mean today," he amended, looking at the clock, "I shall take a post-chaise to Highgate and see if I can secure the premises for us."

They sat for another half an hour, discussing what they would like to call the pub, what they wanted it to be like, and dreaming of the fine clients they would have, until Rainbird reminded them of the hour and said they would never rise in the morning unless they all went immediately to bed.

But for some of the servants, it was an uneasy night.

Lizzie tossed and turned as she thought of marriage to Joseph. She was still fond of Joseph, of course. But marriage! Joseph had seemed such a grand creature in the early days of her employment, when she could barely read or write. But the education of Lizzie, started by a previous tenant, and continued by the staff as a whole, had changed her outlook. After a long time of considering herself of no account, Lizzie was beginning to think she might be worth someone a little kinder and a little less vain than Joseph.

But she had been so much in love with him, and now everyone, including Joseph, had taken their future marriage as an accepted fact. Lizzie thought again of the Comte St. Bertin's valet, Mr. Paul Gendreau, whom she had met when leaving the church earlier that year. He had treated her like a lady; he had been sympathetic. She could not forget him, however hard she tried. But Mr. Gendreau was French, and French servants were even more class-conscious than English ones. It had amused him to be gallant to a scullery maid. He probably never thought of her. A tear rolled down Lizzie's cheek and plopped on the thin blanket that covered her.

Alice, too, was uneasy about her future. She kept seeing Fergus's strong, tanned face. But she would soon be whipped off to freedom and Highgate, the duke would engage other servants, and she would never see Fergus again. She wanted to confide in the chambermaid, Jenny, with whom she shared a bed, but felt she might dim her friend's excitement over the pub.

She would have been surprised had she known that Jenny, too, was uneasy. Somehow, that Miss Jenny Sutherland, having the same first name as her own, had unsettled the chambermaid. It was an unfair world where one Jenny could wear pretty gowns and go to balls and dance with a duke, while she, the servant Jenny, was condemned to a life of servitude. For, Jenny thought gloomily, she would have little chance of marrying anyone interesting while she scrubbed the floors and waited on the customers in the tap. Like Lizzie, she felt she deserved something better in life— something better than the type of man who would propose to a servant in a pub, albeit a servant who owned part of the pub. She would probably get a proposal from one of those uncouth louts who were always on the look-out for a work-horse with some money, a wife to scrub and sew and clean.

In the next room, Joseph lay awake also, flexing his tortured feet under the bedclothes. The servants had been driving single-mindedly towards freedom, and now they were on the threshold. Joseph had always carried in his mind a rosy dream of standing at the entrance to the inn dressed in the latest thing in a buckram-wadded coat, receiving the nobility. He would bow low and hear my lady murmur to her lord, "What an elegant young man."

But now Rainbird was going off to secure the inn—an inn that would require a great deal of manual labour to set it to rights. It was clear that Rainbird meant all of them to help. Joseph raised his hands in front of him and studied their whiteness in the flickering glow of the rushlight. He would not be allowed to wear white gloves or velvet livery. There would be no jaunts to The Running Footman—the pub round the corner where all the upper London servants met to exchange gossip. Highgate was in the country. For the first time Joseph realised his bones were made of pavement. He detested the country, all smells and flies and bumpkins. Of course, Lizzie would be a comfort. But would she? Joseph frowned. Ever since she had become lettered, Lizzie had shown a distressing independence of mind and no longer hung on his every word.

On his pallet under the kitchen table, little Dave settled down to indulge in his favourite fantasy, which was of touring the fairgrounds and taking round the hat after Mr. Rainbird had finished his performance. But the dream no longer comforted him. For the future was right there, and the future was that pub they had all schemed and worked hard to get. "Blow the pub," muttered Dave sulkily. "I hopes we don't get it. I wish Lizzie would do something stupid again." For Lizzie had, earlier that year, become enamoured of the first footman, Luke, who worked for Lord Charteris next door. Luke had persuaded Lizzie to give him all the savings to put on a horse and had promptly run off with the money. But their recent tenant had refunded that money, so there was nothing to stop the buying of the pub now.

Palmer was lucky. The duke had breakfasted well and was in a mellow mood. Angus's coffee, grilled kidneys, and thin slices of toast had been a miracle of cuisine. The day outside was sunny and glorious, and the narrow town house sparkled with cleanliness and comfort. Not by a flicker had any of the servants betrayed anything of the odd events of the night before. The duke had feared they might become cheeky and bold after he had honoured their revels with his august presence.

So Palmer's arrival with the books found the duke singularly uncritical. Rainbird, listening with his ear to the dining-room door, gloomily heard the duke say, "Everything appears to be in order, Palmer, although I still maintain the servants here are paid too low a wage."

"They are well content with what they get," Rainbird heard Palmer reply gruffly.

So that was that, thought Rainbird, unaware that the duke had been looking at a list of wages that were much higher than the pittance Palmer actually gave them. Rainbird assumed Palmer had therefore not fiddled the books, and so they had no way of getting even with him. Better to see about that pub and then hand in their notices.

When Palmer had left, the duke summoned Rainbird and told him that he would spend the afternoon with friends who lived at Primrose Hill, have dinner with them, and return in the evening to change for the Denbys' musicale. Still feeling happy, the duke grandly told Rainbird the servants might enjoy some free time, provided they were on hand in the evening to attend to his needs.

Fergus, who was to accompany his master, went down to the servants' hall to say goodbye. He felt envious of the servants, who were eagerly making plans for the day. Rainbird alone did not voice his plans. How lovely it would be, thought Fergus wistfully, to be able to invite the glorious Alice to go out walking in the parks.

Lizzie had planned to go to St. Patrick's Church in Soho Square, trying to persuade herself she had been sadly lacking in her religious duties, but hoping all the while for a glimpse of Mr. Gendreau. Alice and Jenny were going to look at the shops, Angus and Mrs. Middleton were to take a walk by the Serpentine, Joseph was going to The Running Footman for a gossip, and Dave announced firmly he was going with Rainbird.

They all waited eagerly until they heard the duke and Fergus leave, and then they set about preparing to enjoy the day.

Rainbird hired a post-chaise, took the strong-box with their money, and, accompanied by Dave, set out for Highgate. The day was so fine and so sparkling that Rainbird wished they could have afforded to hire an open carriage instead of being confined inside a stuffy, smelly post-chaise.

The inn called The Holly Bush was on the far side of Highgate, on the north road out of that village. It was owned, among other run-down properties, by a certain Squire James, who lived in the village. He was a gross, slovenly man, who showed alarming signs of wishing to show them about in person, swearing the place was double the money. But Rainbird said firmly they would judge matters better on their own and would return shortly and let him know their decision.

Having dismissed the post-chaise, they walked out to The Holly Bush. It was a Tudor pub with a thatched roof. To Rainbird's surprise, the thatch was in good repair and the glass in all the windows was unbroken. But inside, the tap was a squalid, disgusting mess. It looked as if there had been an almighty brawl on its last night, and no one had bothered to clean it up. There were four bedrooms upstairs. There was a weedy garden at the back with a muddy pond choked with reeds. But to Rainbird's surprise, the fabric of the building was sound, and the floors were good and solid. The pond could be cleaned, and tables and chairs could be arranged in the garden. Short of cleaning and scrubbing inside, there would be remarkably little to be done to get it ready.

Much cheered, Rainbird and Dave made their way back to the squire's. Squire James was smelling strongly of freshly taken brandy when they went in. Rainbird, with a long and solemn face, immediately began to run down the pub and complain about the mess. The squire protested furiously and told them to go. Rainbird hummed and hawed and said he might consider buying it if the squire would take hard cash and dispense with the formality of lawyers, who were a useless and expensive breed, a sentiment with which the squire heartily agreed.

Rainbird sat down with the squire and an hour of haggling ensued, until Rainbird clinched the deal by producing bags of guineas from the strong-box and letting them spill out on the table. As he saw the squire's eyes light up greedily at the sight of the gold, Rainbird was glad he had changed all their notes into guineas. Paper money never inspired the same greed in men as did the sight of gold. And so the squire eagerly sold the pub for a lesser sum that he had first demanded. The papers and documents were handed over and all the spare keys.

Rainbird walked away with a light heart. Down below them swam London in a soft golden haze, like a magic city in a dream.

"A good day's work, Dave," said Rainbird cheerfully, "and money still in hand. Come, my lad, and we will have food and drink somewhere pleasant."

They settled for a pub called The Grenadier, soon to be their rival, and had a meal of cold roast beef and porter out in the inn garden under the cool shade of a chestnut tree.

"Will you entertain the customers, Mr. Rainbird?" asked Dave wistfully.

"No, I shall be a pompous landlord, mine host to the life." Rainbird leapt to his feet and strutted up and down the grass, pushing out an imaginary paunch.

Dave crowed with laughter. "There's no one but us in the garden, Mr. Rainbird," he leaded. "Do some of your tricks."

Rainbird shrugged and smiled. He picked some walnuts from a bowl on the table and began to juggle them. "Can you imagine the Duke of Pelham behaving thus?" Rainbird laughed. He fixed Dave with a haughty, glacial eye and then glared at the circle of juggled walnuts with horror, as if wondering how they had got into his hands. He mimed a pompous aristocrat desperately trying to get rid of the offending things while little Dave wiped his tears of laughter away on his sleeve.

Rainbird tossed the walnuts back in the bowl and then cart-wheeled round the garden, finishing upside down on the table-top, legs straight up in the air, propped up on one hand.

The sound of applause from the doorway leading to the garden made Rainbird jump back into his seat and assume the expression of a man who had absolutely nothing to do with the antics he had just performed.

"My dear sir," said a fat, florid, and jolly man who had been applauding. "You could rival Grimaldi." Grimaldi was the famous clown of the Regency patnomime.

"With your permission?" Without waiting for a reply, the man sat down at the table. "I am stage manager of the Spa Theatre in Islington. I am also the owner. We are sadly in need of a harlequin for our pantomime. If you would be consider joining our band of players, I would pay you well."

Rainbird smiled and shook his head. Harlequins were at the bottom of the theatrical scale. He had read in the newspapers recently that Grimaldi himself could only earn four pounds a week.

"You are kind, Mr. ——?"

"Frank."

"Mr. Frank. I have just bought a pub. I am a gentleman of independent means, and harlequins earn too little to tempt me."

"Nonsense, Mr. ——?"

"Rainbird. John Rainbird."

"You will make your name. You can earn generous sums of money touring the provinces, as much as fourteen thousand pounds in four weeks and one hundred pounds on benefit nights. If you joined our troupe, you could count on a percentage of the takings as well."

"It seems a great sum for a few tricks."

"Few have the ability to make others laugh. You have what I want, what I need, Mr. John Rainbird. What! Slave in a pub and never hear the roar of the audience in your ears?"

"Oh, Mr. Rainbird," breathed Dave. "There's enough o' the others to run the pub."

Rainbird shook his head. "I have duty to my friends to consider," he said. "Besides, I might prove a failure."

Mr. Frank hitched his chair closer. "Just one night," he wheedled. "You could try one night. It's not as if there are any lines to rehearse."

The theatrical performances of the Regency were very long, about five or six hours, and the play was always followed by a harlequinade in which Harlequin danced in pursuit of Columbine, was opposed by Pantaloon, but finally, with the aid of his wooden sword or bat, defeated his enemies and won the girl. There was always a comic chase, and Harlequin was expected to entertain the audience with tricks and juggling and songs and a running patter on the events of the day.

Rainbird looked around the sunny garden. It would be wonderful to perform in a theatre before he settled down. Just once.

"I am at the moment butler to the Duke of Pelham. My time is his. It would be very hard to escape for the evening. Which evening had you in mind?"

"Sooner the better. You pick your evening. The harlequin we have is old and drunk. You turn up and we'll take him off for the night."

Rainbird bit his knuckles in sudden agitation. "But to walk onto a stage in front of all these people with a cast who do not even know me!"

"You make 'em laugh, and they won't care what you do. The audience, I mean. You make 'em laugh, and the cast will just have to try to follow you."

"Let me think about it," said Rainbird. Dave looked at him anxiously. The butler had turned quite white and his hands shook.

"Do that, Mr. Rainbird. Here is my card. What have you to lose? If you are a success, the world lies before you. If you fail, then you go to your pub and forget about it."

He clapped Rainbird on the shoulder and ambled off.

Rainbird stared down at the card. "Oh dear," he whispered to Dave. "Whatever shall I do? You never think a dream will ever become reality. To dream about going on the stage is one thing, but to actually have that dream here in my grasp, and not to be able to hold it, is very hard. I wish we had never met Mr. Frank. I shall make a very discontented landlord."

Dave put a grubby hand on Rainbird's sleeve. "Please, Mr. Rainbird," he said, "try just one night. I'll come along 'o you. Dave'll be there. Please, Mr. Rainbird. Like the man said, you can try the one evening. One evening's not much."

Joseph, in black-and-gold livery and with his hair powdered, strolled in the direction of The Running Footman. He walked with his constricted feet pointing outwards like a fencing master. In one white-gloved hand he carried a lace-edged handkerchief. His blue eyes surveyed the world with pleasure. He rounded the corner of Clarges Street and nearly bumped into Miss Jenny Sutherland, who was returning home from a shopping expedition accompanied by her maid, Cooper.

Joseph bowed slightly and would have walked past, not

wanting to embarrass Miss Sutherland, but to his surprise Jenny stopped dead and hailed him with a cheerful "Good day, Joseph. How goes it?"

"Very well," said Joseph, noticing the startled look on the maid's face.

"Take my packages home, Cooper," said Jenny. "Oh, don't look so shocked. I shall follow you directly."

When the maid had reluctantly walked away, Jenny said, "Last night your master appeared to be quite a different gentleman from the one I first met. Not at all proud."

Rainbird would have told Miss Sutherland firmly that she was in danger of disgracing herself by standing talking to servants in the street, but Joseph had such a high opinion of himself that he saw nothing wrong in it, although all the glory of chatting with a supremely beautiful lady of fashion went right to his head.

"He's proud enough to keep us et stervation level," said the gossipy Joseph, enjoying the startled look of curiosity in Jenny's eyes. Jenny's stopping to talk to Joseph was part of her new plan to take an interest in others, no matter who they might be.

"What do you mean?" she asked. "Are your wages so very low?"

Joseph outlined how little they all got. "But that is shocking . . . shocking," said Jenny.

"Mind you," said Joseph, "Mr. Rainbird says es how he thinks thet Palmer, the duke's agent, is cheating his mester. He thinks thet Palmer gives us one set of wages, marks higher ones in the duke's books, and pockets the difference." Rainbird had not told the others about what he had heard going on between Palmer and the duke, for he had temporarily forgotten about it in the excitement of setting out with Dave to see the pub.

"I shall speak to the duke," said Jenny firmly.

"No, don't do thet, miss," said Joseph, alarmed. "See 'ere, it's like this," he said, forgetting his genteel accent. "If we could find a way of getting proof on paper of what he was actually paying us, and have a look at them books, or somethink like that, then we could tell the duke about Palmer. But what if it's really the duke hisself who is paying them low wages?"

"You must break into this Palmer's office and steal his books!" cried Jenny.

"Naw!" squawked Joseph. "I wasn't supposed to talk about it. You wont' tell anyone, miss?"

"Oh, fiddle, there's Cooper coming for me." Jenny hurried off down the street.

Joseph looked after her, feeling awkward and uneasy. Then he reassured himself with the hope that Miss Sutherland would forget about the whole thing.

By the time he pushed open the door of The Running Footman—pausing on the threshold so that the upper servants in the tap should behold the full glory of lace handkerchief, shining pumps, and white silk stockings—Joseph had forgotten about his encounter with Miss Sutherland.

"Over here, Joseph," called a familiar voice. Joseph preened. Mr. Blenkinsop, Lord Charteris's butler from next door, was waving to him. Casting a covert look round to make sure the other footmen in the pub knew he was being invited by a butler, Joseph minced up to where Blenkinsop was sitting, and slid gracefully into the chair opposite.

Mr. Blenkinsop was more what Joseph considered a butler should be—fat and portly and not very clever. Rainbird had often too sharp a tongue for Joseph's comfort.

"What will you have, Joseph?" asked Mr. Blenkinsop expansively.

"A pint of shrub, an' it please you, Mr. Blenkinsop," said Joseph, much gratified, for butlers like Blenkinsop usually expected the lower orders to pay for *their* drinks.

When Joseph had been served, Mr. Blenkinsop said, "We never heard no more word o' that rascal, Luke."

Joseph's face darkened. "Running off wiff all o' our money like that," he said furiously. "'E deserves to be 'anged."

The footman then blushed. He could never understand why his genteel accents, so carefully cultivated, should suddenly run away and leave him with a cockney whine.

"He'll come to a bad end, never fear," said Mr. Blenkinsop, burying his nose in his pewter mug of light ale. His weak eyes then peered craftily over the top of the mug at Joseph. "We ain't got a first footman," he added.

"I thought the next-in-line would have got the job," said Joseph.

Mr. Blenkinsop put down his mug and prodded Joseph in the region of the waistcoat with a fat finger. "None of them have got it," he said. "I need a first footman with a certain jenny-say-quite."

"Exactly," said Joseph.

"A chap like yourself, for example, would fit the post."

"Lord Charteris would never let you take me on," said Joseph. "I may as well tell you, Mr. Blenkinsop, as I know how you can keep a secret, that Palmer, the duke's agent, says as how he would give me a bad reference and tell any employer how it was me what stole from the Bishop of Burnham. But it wasn't," said Joseph passionately. "It was that wife o' his."

Blenkinsop laughed, a fat, chuckling laugh. "Don't everyone know about her?" he said. "Why, only t' other week she had a snuff-box offa Lord Charteris. He knows she steals."

"What!" screeched Joseph, red with outrage. "Here's me bin starvin' for years in that slum in Clarges Street on the worst wages a footman could have, and all because I thought no one knew about the bishop's wife's stealing."

"You ain't done too bad," said Benkinsop, cynically regarding the footman's expensive livery.

"Well, we was lucky with the tenants," admitted Joseph reluctantly. "That why we's all going to buy this pub." Then he went red as fire again, and pleaded, "I shouldn't have told you. Don't tell Mr. Rainbird or he'll thrash me."

"It's my opinion," said Blenkinsop, "that a man like John Rainbird don't appreciate the delicate feelings of a chap like yourself."

"That's true. Very true," said Joseph.

"But if you're all going to be independent and buy pubs, well, there's no point in offering you a job."

"It's very tempting," said Joseph. "I would like to be a first footman."

Blenkinsop leaned back in his chair and watched the battle going on behind Joseph's wide blue eyes. He had no intention of telling Joseph that he, Joseph, had caught the wandering eye of that raddled old harridan, Lady Charteris, and it was my lady who had suggested Joseph should be engaged as first footman.

Unlike the others, Joseph had not come to be discontented with his life as a servant, only with the fact he did not have any proper status in that democratic servants' hall in Clarges Street. But in a house such as Lord Charteris's he would have all the respect due to his position from the other servants. He would be waited on by the lower servants. Lord and Lady Charteris went about in society, and

Lady Charteris liked to have the most senior footman always in attendance. Damn the pub, thought Joseph. He would need to ruin his hands and suffer that affectionate, contemptuous look in Rainbird's eyes and see Lizzie drifting farther away from him—pulled away from him by a long chain of books. Like many of his betters, Joseph was inclined to think that education for the lower orders was a dangerous thing.

"If only I could," he said.

"What's the arrangement with this pub, then?" asked Blenkinsop.

"Well, we're all equal partners," said Joseph.

"That's very fair of John Rainbird."

"I s'pose," said Joseph reluctantly. "But I hates the country, and this pub is in Highgate," he said as if Highgate were in Outer Mongolia.

"You're like me, lad." Blenkinsop sighed. "I like a London life. We remove to the country in the winter, mind. But we're treated well and we're never expected to poke our noses outdoors. They've got plenty of outdoor staff. Besides, I'll be retiring soon and that'll leave my job vacant. It would be fine to be able to train my successor."

Joseph's round eyes grew rounder.

"See here," said Blenkinsop. "You could always let them have your share of the money. Tell 'em, if the pub succeeds, to put a little bit by for you. Look on it as an investment. They don't need you. There's plenty o' them to run it as it is."

Mrs. Middleton walked sedately along by the Serpentine with the cook, Angus MacGregor. Although all this idea of a pub of their own was very exciting, it left one great black hole in the housekeeper's ambitions. The "Mrs." was a courtesy title. Daughter of an impoverished country curate, Mrs. Middleton was a spinster who had long dreamt of being married to Mr. John Rainbird when they all had their independence. But Mr. Rainbird, she realised with a sigh, showed no signs of wanting to be married to her, or indeed anyone. Not these days. Not since he had made a fool of himself over some useless French lady's maid who had not wanted him.

"Weel, we'll soon be free," she realised Angus MacGregor was saying.

"Yes, it seems strange," she said. "I once read of a man who had spent years in a debtor's prison, and when friends finally raised the money to get him out, he was so bewildered and lost in the world outside that he gambled and gambled until he was back in prison again. I wonder whether I shall feel like that."

"I wouldnae want to be married to a lady who craved to remain a servant all her days," said the cook severely.

"What!" screamed Mrs. Middleton, shocked into rudeness.

"I have a terrible temper," said the cook mournfully, "and I'm aye doing things the wrong way. But let me see if I can get this right."

He sat the bewildered housekeeper down on a park bench next to the shining water, took out a clean handkerchief, dropped it on the ground, and knelt down on one knee in front of her.

"Mistress Middleton," said Angus MacGregor, "will you marry me?"

Mrs. Middleton blinked and looked over his head at the shining water. All the colours of the day seemed sharp and incredibly bright, and from somewhere above the clouds drifted down the triumphant fanfare of trumpets.

"Oh, yes, Angus," she said.

"That's all right then," said the cook, jumping to his feet. "Now, we're engaged, ye may take ma arm."

Mrs. Middleton rose and shook out her skirts and allowed Angus to tuck her arm in his. She felt very young and weak and feminine. She looked shyly up at the cook, her face radiant, her frightened lines and wrinkles for the moment erased.

Angus squeezed her arm. "Ah'm telling you," he said, "we'll run the best pub wi' the best food in the whole of England.

"Yes, we will, won't we?" said Mrs. Middleton, quite breathless with happiness.

Lizzie had said her prayers. She had tried to concentrate and keep her mind above worldly things. But she still felt miserable. Why she had expected Paul Gendreau to be standing in the same church on the very day she had decided to visit it, she did not know. But the fact that the French valet was not there had left her feeling sick with disappointment.

She was about to leave when she realised that if God saw everything, he must surely know the thoughts in one little scullery maid's head. There could be no harm in asking. So Lizzie, down on her knees again, trustingly asked God to let her see Paul Gendreau again, if it should be His will.

She left the church feeling a little comforted. She was wearing a pretty leaf-green muslin gown that had been bought for her by a previous tenant. Her brown hair was washed and brushed and confined by a cherry-red silk ribbon, the first present she had ever received. She stood blinking in the sunlight after the darkness of the church, reluctant to go straight back to Clarges Street. Then she remembered that the French emigrés who had managed to smuggle out enough wealth to maintain a position had set up a sort of Faubourg St. Honoré in and around Manchester Square. It was a pleasant day for a walk. And there would be no harm in just going for a look . . .

Soon she was turning off Oxford Street and into Duke Street, which led to Manchester Square. She began to hear the sound of French voices all about her. Feeling quite bold, now she had ventured this far, she stopped first one and then the other when she reached Manchester Square, asking for the direction of the Comte St. Bertin. But the servants she stopped spoke no English; French servants, like their masters, often despising their host country and refusing to speak English if by chance they knew any. At last, she hit upon an English coachman who was just climbing down from the box of his carriage.

"The Comte lived over there, miss," said the coachman. "But if you was wanting to see him, you're too late."

He pointed with his whip to a tall house that had a hatchment over the door and a mute wailing on the steps.

Lizzie looked at the shuttered windows and her heart sank.

Despite herself, she walked slowly round the square until she was standing in front of the house. Perhaps she would not have been able to recognise Mr. Gendreau, even if she had seen him again, she thought. The night she had met him had been dark and rainy and she had only caught glimpses of his face in the weak light of the parish lamps in Clarges Street.

"Excuse me, miss," said a voice at her ear. "But I have this odd feeling we have met before."

Lizzie started and turned about. She recognised Paul

Gendreau immediately, although he was more richly dressed than she had remembered, and his eyes were sharper and bolder.

"You walked me home from the church one evening," said Lizzie timidly.

"Ah, yes, Clarges Street. The little scullery maid. I remember.

Lizzie dropped her eyes. Somehow that phrase "little scullery maid" had dashed all her dreams.

She rallied. "I am sorry your master is dead."

Mr. Gendreau spread his hands and gave a very Gallic shrug. "He was very old, and it was expected. There is sadness in your eyes. Why? Not for me, I trust. Milord has left me a tidy sum in his will. *Voilà!* Before you now stands Paul Gendreau, gentleman."

"I am happy for you," said Lizzie quietly. She started to walk away. This ebullient and confident Mr. Gendreau was not the quiet, attentive valet she remembered. He fell into step beside her.

"And why are you at liberty this free day, Miss O' Brien?"

"You remember my name?" exclaimed Lizzie.

"Yes, of course."

"The owner of the house where I work, the Duke of Pelham, is in residence. He has given us the day off."

"An unusual aristocrat. Usually they like to think of us slaving while they take their pleasures."

"Was your master like that?"

"Very. He was a French aristocrat of the old school. Me, I am a royalist, but sometimes I used to look at him and say to myself, 'Now I see why there was a revolution in France.' "

They had reached the corner of Manchester Square.

Lizzie curtsied again. "Goodbye, Mr. Gendreau," she said politely. "I have enjoyed meeting you again."

"Goodbye!" he echoed. "Here we are on a beautiful day, both free. Nonsense. We shall proceed to Gunter's and have ices."

"Gunter's!" squeaked Lizzie. "Only ladies and gentlemen go to Gunter's." Gunter's was the famous confectioner in Berkeley Square.

"But you are wearing a modish gown, and me, I am dressed like a gentleman. I have saved and saved for years, and now I do not need my savings, for milord has left me plenty of money. Come, Miss O'Brien."

He tried to cajole Lizzie into speech as they walked across Oxford Street, but Lizzie was sure that as soon as they entered Gunter's, they would be asked to leave. But they were ushered with all courtesy to a table and the amused Paul Gendreau, seeing Lizzie was too frightened to open her mouth, ordered a strawberry ice cream for her and one for himself.

"Now, Miss Lizzie," he said, "no one is going to chase us away. No one is looking at us. Tell me why you look so sad."

His clever eyes were warm and sympathetic. Lizzie began in bits and pieces to tell him about the pub and how the prospect of freedom was making her afraid, that she often wondered whether the others would treat her like one of the owners of the pub, or forget, and continue to treat her as a scullery maid. At times she fell silent, but, prompted by his questions, she proceeded to tell him all about Palmer, about the previous tenants, about how she was expected to marry Joseph, and how she did not love Joseph anymore. At last she stopped in confusion, having never in her life before talked so much about herself.

"You must marry whom you please," he said gently. "We servants are not allowed to marry, and when we get our freedom we should have the luxury of marrying whom we please."

"But they all expect me to marry Joseph!"

"When you think of marriage," he asked, "how do you picture it?"

"I suppose it may seem silly to you," said Lizzie slowly, looking at his neat worldly features and clever eyes, "but I always wanted a little place in the country and a garden and some land. I've always wanted some gentleman to care for, someone who would also care for me."

Lizzie heaved a great sigh and a large tear rolled down her cheek and plopped into the melting remains of the strawberry ice on her plate. He took out a handkerchief and dabbed her wet cheek.

"It is not silly," he said. "Not right in the country, of course, but near enough to some town to have the pleasures of both. I like Bath. There are many pretty villages quite near so that one may have the pleasures of concerts and coffee rooms and bookshops, and yet enjoy the clean air of the country. I saw such a house once. He pulled out a notebook and lead pencil. "See, it looked like this." He sketched rapidly. "Two stories and a good tiled roof. I do not like the thatch. Insanitary. Plenty of windows for light, but not too many or the window tax would cripple me. A square of garden at the front, like so. And shaded by some fine elms. And roses! Red and white, over the door . . . here. And at the back, a good vegetable garden. And beyond the hedge here . . ." He looked up impatiently at a hovering waiter. "No, my good man, we are not finished. Bring us tea and a selection of cakes and take yourself off. Where was

I? Ah yes, and beyond the hedge, a pasture where one could keep, say, two cows, a horse, and perhaps a pig."

"And inside? What was it like inside?" asked Lizzie.

"I never saw the inside. But I would have it so." He turned to a clean page of the notebook.

"A dining room here on this side and a living room on the other side of the hall. A big kitchen. Probably the present one would have to be extended. Four bedrooms above, and two small ones in the attics. And if there were space enough, I would put in a room with a bath with running water. They have them now with a machine at the head of the bathtub which can supply hot water."

"It would be quite a lot to keep clean," said Lizzie.

"But I should have servants, of course. No butler, no footmen, *vous voyez,* but a cook-housekeeper and two stout maids, and a man to do the rough outside work. Then nothing grand in the way of a carriage, but a gig and horse to take me into Bath."

Tea and cakes were placed in front of them. Lizzie poured tea correctly as she had seen the fine ladies do, and treasured every moment of her outing.

"The pub Mr. Rainbird has chosen for us is in Highgate," said Lizzie. "But if you are going to Bath, it is unlikely you will journey that far."

"When will you be free?" he asked abruptly.

"When Mr. Rainbird says so," said Lizzie. "Not very long now. The end of the Season at the latest."

"That is not very far away."

"No," said Lizzie sadly. She put one of Gunter's finest cakes, half-eaten, down on her plate and wondered why it suddenly tasted like dust.

He put his elbows on the table and studied her. "I have

never before met a lady quite like yourself, Miss Lizzie," he said. "Such prettiness—such humility."

Lizzie looked up quickly to see if he were laughing at her, but his eyes were serious.

"Go on about your house," said Lizzie. "I like hearing about it."

He opened the notebook again, and then said slowly, "What kind of furniture shall we have in the living room?"

"*We*, Mr. Gendreau?"

"Yes, we. There is that between us which is already very precious. When I talk about my dream house, I see you there, and you see yourself there, is that not so?"

Lizzie went very still. "I am a good Catholic, Mr. Gendreau, and I could not countenance . . ."

"Anything other than marriage. Of course not. I should not be proposing to you if I thought you were the sort of lady who would settle for anything less. Stop staring at me like that, chérie, and let us get down to the practicals. Now, me, I do not like this fashion for backless sofas . . ."

"There's one life for some Jennys and one life for the others," said Jenny, the chambermaid, suddenly, stopping dead in the middle of the Strand.

"Whatever do you mean?" asked Alice.

"Never mind," said fierce little Jenny.

The object of her envy, Miss Jenny Sutherland, sat in front of her glass that evening with her eyes tightly closed as Cooper dressed her hair.

Would it not be wonderful, thought Jenny, to break into Palmer's office and find those books? That would prove to herself and everyone else that she was not selfish. She must find out where Palmer's office was.

"Why ever has you got your eyes closed?" asked Cooper, twirling the curling tongs.

"Because things look better that way," said Miss Jenny Sutherland.

Chapter
Five

If all the good people were clever,
And all clever people were good,
The world would be nicer than ever
We thought that it possibly could.

But somehow, 'tis seldom or never
The two hit it off as they should;
The good are so harsh to the clever,
The clever so rude to the good!

—Elizabeth Wordsworth

"Everything all right belowstairs?" asked
the Duke of Pelham, as he dressed that
evening.

"Yes, your grace," said Fergus. "Have the servants
been annoying your grace?"

"No, as correct as ever. But the atmosphere of this
house has changed. It is very hard to explain. There is a
restless, unhappy feeling."

Fergus looked about uneasily. "Perhaps it is the spirit
of the late duke."

"It feels more like the spirit of present and living unhappiness. Rainbird, that normally confident butler, appears uneasy, restless, and abstracted; the beauty of a blonde maid—what is her name. . . . ?"

"Alice."

"Yes, Alice. She looks sad. The little chambermaid has eyes red from recent weeping and performs her duties in a state of suppressed rage. The effeminate Joseph is correct to a fault and goes about his business with an air, but he occasionally flashes sidelong looks of dislike at his butler—a butler who, only yesterday, I could have sworn, was regarded in the light of father of this household."

"They were all up late last night," said Fergus. "They are probably tired. And then they have all been out all day."

"Perhaps it was wrong of me to give them a day off. My friends, the Chesters at Primrose Hill, were quite shocked when I happened to mention the matter. Servants, they told me, are allowed two days off a year. Any other arrangement leads to laziness and deceit. But I cannot see the wisdom of keeping servants belowstairs in this beautiful weather when I do not need them. Unhealthy servants, like unhealthy troops, are of no use to me whatsoever. Was I too lenient? Are they discontented?"

"I did not notice anything wrong," said Fergus. Alice had smiled at him warmly, and so he had not noticed anything else. If Alice smiled at him, then Fergus thought that everything must be right with the whole wide world.

And it surely showed some change must have taken place in his haughty master's flinty soul that he should concern himself with his servants. But the duke now regarded servants in the same way as he had regarded his troops. The men who had fought under him in the Peninsula had found him a good leader, for he kept a sharp eye out for their welfare. Now he was back in civilian life, he had kept this faculty of noticing the temperament of those who worked under him. But there was something else.

The peaceful, restful family atmosphere of the house had been shattered. Unrest was in the very air. The duke, on the journey back from Primrose Hill, had quite decided not to go to the Denbys' musicale, but to stay quietly at home and relax. But the strung-up air that haunted the tall building had communicated its restlessness to him, and he had found himself ordering Fergus to lay out his evening clothes.

He wondered if little Miss Sutherland would be at the musicale, and then dismissed her from his mind. She was too young and too flighty. She had been charming last night, but no doubt would prove to be as vain and spoilt as ever if he should see her again.

Mrs. Freemantle was late getting dressed, and so most of the guests were seated at the musicale by the time Jenny arrived with her two chaperones. They had to sit at the very back.

She barely heard any of the music, so engrossed was she in plans to help the servants of Number 67. It was only when the concert was over and everyone rose to move through to the supper room that she became aware of the other guests. She saw the Duke of Pelham and smiled faintly and received a rather frosty nod in return.

Lady Letitia, Mrs. Freemantle, and Jenny were joined at supper by Lord Paul Mannering. He was very courteous and amusing, talking about plays and operas and the gossip of the day. His eyes occasionally rested with approval on Jenny's demure face. But Jenny was glancing here and there under her long lashes. She saw Miss Maddox, she of the pug-face, sitting next to a young gentleman who appeared highly amused by her company. Then Miss Maddox spilled a little wine on her gown and dabbed at it ineffectually with her handkerchief. She made a funny grimace of distress and then rose to her feet.

With a breathless "Excuse me," Jenny rose also and hurried out of the room after Miss Maddox.

She found her in an ante-room that had been set aside for the ladies' toilet. A maid was sponging Miss Maddox's gown with soda water.

Jenny fiddled with her hair and wondered how to start a conversation, but Miss Maddox looked at her and grinned. "Dreadful stuff, red wine," she said. "Such a tiny little bit of it seems to go so far."

"Anything spilled seems to increase in volume," said Jenny. "A cup of water becomes a Niagara when it is spilled on the floor. May I introduce myself? I am Miss Jenny Sutherland, but lately come to town."

"And I am Miss Mary Maddox," said the other, holding out her hand. "How d'ye do."

"Very well, I thank you."

"And how are you enjoying London?" asked Miss Maddox, dismissing her maid with a wave of her hand.

"I have not yet seen much of it," said Jenny. "I did see you the other night at the Bessamys' party."

"Oh, yes. I remember seeing you. How I danced! My poor feet still ache."

"I did not dance at all," said Jenny bitterly. "I fear my looks are not fashionable."

"Did you not know what happened?" cried Mary Maddox. "It was all Pelham's fault, of course."

"Pelham! What had he to do with it?"

"Did not Mrs. Bessamy tell you? She was so incensed

and called him cruel. The duke told that rattle, Mr. Camden, that no gentleman of fashion should be seen dancing with you, and gossipy Mr. Camden told the other gentlemen."

Jenny took a deep breath. "I could kill him," she raged.

"Tonight he was denying the whole thing and saying that Miss Sutherland was remarkably pretty and bound to be all the rage."

"I wonder if my aunt, Lady Letitia, knew of this," said Jenny. "But she could not, for she said it was all my own fault."

"Is Lady Letitia the extremely modish lady who is with you and Mrs. Freemantle?"

Jenny nodded.

"I do not think so. For she appeared distressed and puzzled. I should not worry about stuffy Pelham. You are vastly pretty. Everyone says so."

Jenny looked in the glass. The old, familiar vain Jenny looked back. It was like meeting a dear friend again. Jenny's eyes began to sparkle.

"I am much indebted to you, Miss Maddox, for your news."

"Will you not call me Mary? I feel we might be friends."

Before Jenny could reply, Lady Letitia and Mrs. Freemantle came into the room. "I must pin up Agnes' hem," said Lady Letitia. "Go back and entertain Lord Paul, Jenny, until we return."

Jenny darted off without staying to introduce Mary Maddox. Lady Letitia introduced herself and apologised for her charge's thoughtlessness.

"I am afraid I gave Miss Sutherland a shock," said

Mary. "I told her what the Duke of Pelham had been saying about her."

"Oh dear," boomed Mrs. Freemantle. "Now she will be swanning and preening all over the place."

Mary gave the older ladies a puzzled look, but Lady Letitia merely compressed her lips, took a reel of silk and a needle out of her reticule, and bent to the task of stitching the hem of Mrs. Freemantle's gown.

Mary Maddox returned to her supper companion, a Mr. Toby Parry. Mr. Parry was a fresh-faced young man with a mop of golden curls and a nose as undistinguished and snub as Mary's own. His grey eyes lit up at the sight of her.

"I have been talking to London's latest beauty, Miss Jenny Sutherland."

"You mean the young lady with the dark hair over there with Lord Paul? The one Pelham did not like?"

"Yes. I hope we can be friends. I found her charming and unaffected."

"Would you say she was really unaffected?" asked Toby Parry. Miss Sutherland was undoubtedly very beautiful, but he thought the way she was flashing beguiling looks at Lord Paul, a man old enough to be her father, was a trifle bold, to say the least.

"Oh yes. I am quite determined to call on her. Perhaps she would care to go driving with me tomorrow."

"I would be ready to escort you," said Toby eagerly.

"Aha!" laughed Mary. "She has enslaved you already."

"Not I!" exclaimed Toby, alarmed. "My affections are engaged elsewhere."

"Now who can the lucky lady be? I wonder. Here is Mr. Angers come to join us."

Toby threw the newcomer a smouldering glare, and then sat with his arms folded, looking decidedly sulky as Mary turned and began chatting to Mr. Angers.

"Before your aunt returns, Miss Sutherland," Lord Paul was saying, "I crave your indulgence. Do you believe in love at first sight?"

Jenny gave him a startled look, and then a slow, warm smile. "I believe such a thing exists outside books, my lord, yes."

Lord Paul took a deep breath. "Then it will not surprise you to learn I am desirous of joining my name with that of your family. I shall call at Clarges Street at noon tomorrow. Here is Lady Letitia. No more of this at present."

Jenny leaned back in her chair and looked across the room. She was bathed in a radiant glow of triumph. Two days in London and already she was to receive a proposal of marriage. Lord Paul was talking to Lady Letitia, leaning forward and smiling into her aunt's eyes. Jenny was only barely aware of them. Her eyes met those of the Duke of Pelham, and she threw him an amused smile. How furious he would be to learn that his friend had fallen victim to such indistinguished charms. Of course she would accept Lord Paul. He was old, but he was kind and handsome and a tremendous catch.

Now what is making that little minx so happy all of a sudden? wondered the duke before turning back to his companion. He had taken Lady Clarissa Bellisle into supper. She was a cool and stately widow in her late twenties. She had reddish-brown hair, fashionably styled, a long thin nose, a full mouth, and rather protruding liquid brown eyes. Her gown of brown-and-gold-shot silk revealed an excellent figure. As the duke did not believe in love, and was already fatigued at the prospect of hunting for a wife, he felt he had been very lucky indeed to meet Lady Bellisle so soon. He would need to make inquiries about her background and fortune, but his lawyers could be entrusted to do that. Provided there were no scandals in her past, he felt sure she would make him a very good wife. She was sophisticated and witty, and although she showed perhaps too much interest in the more vulgar side of the theatre—she claimed the clown, Grimaldi, was a genius—there was nothing else about her to give him a disgust of her. That he might be expected to flirt a little, send her flowers, or show some warmth did not enter the duke's head. He knew his worth. Any lady would be glad to have him, particularly a widow.

Lady Bellisle was complaining about the difficulty of finding good servants. The duke told her he was thinking of putting the Clarges Street town house on the market and recommended the servants. "I can contrive to find places for some," he added. "But they are a close-knit bunch and I cannot imagine them ever working in separate establishments. I gave them the day off today because I did not need their services, but friends of mine told me it was a silly thing to do and that servants should not be allowed extra time off."

"I have given mine the evening off," said Lady Bellisle, "apart from my maid, coachman, and footmen. The kitchen staff live too much of their life below ground, and if they are not allowed up into the fresh air, then they sicken and that can cost a great deal in physician's bills. Mine are inclined to be lazy, but I have a good butler who contrives to keep them in order. But I do not see the point in keeping servants tied to the house when one has no need of them. An interest in the welfare of servants is now unfashionable but very important. It is dangerous to leave them too long to their own discontented thoughts. It is important to know at all times what ails them and whether they are unhappy. Otherwise, they might leave, and then one is put to the fatiguing job of supervising the training of new maids."

"So you do not think I did wrong," said the duke, "by allowing my own bunch of peculiars unexpected liberty?"

"Not in the slightest."

"Perhaps I should ask them if anything is troubling them," he said half to himself. "I can hardly begin to explain, Lady Bellisle, how wonderful and happy the atmosphere of my house was this morning and how changed and restless this evening."

"I suppose I could speak to them for you, your grace, if it would please you."

"I can deal with them myself, but it would please me greatly to see more of you, Lady Bellisle. May I take you driving at five tomorrow?" Five o'clock was the fashionable hour for driving in the Park.

She hesitated. The duke frowned horribly. Lady Bellisle would most certainly sink in his opinion of her if she did not realise the full honour that was being done to her.

"Yes, your grace," she said finally. "I should like that above all things."

Before leaving the Denbys, Mary Maddox secured Lady Letitia's permission to take Jenny driving. "A very prettily behaved miss," said Lady Letitia as Mary walked away.

"Yes, and she told me the most monstrous thing!" cried Jenny. "Pelham deliberately tried to ruin me socially."

"So I believe," said Lady Letitia repressively.

Jenny looked shocked. "And yet you said all those unkind things!"

"I did not know then about Pelham, and when I learned about his behaviour—behaviour he has been at pains to put right; he told several gossipy gentlemen tonight he had said no such thing and that you were a diamond of the first water. As I was saying, when I learned of his behaviour, I did not tell you because I feared you would grow vain again. You were badly in need of a set-down, however cruel it may have seemed at the time."

Jenny was furious. "I may as well tell you, Aunt," she said, "that not everyone has such a low opinion of me as you. In fact, you may not bother your head about my future any longer. Lord Paul Mannering is to call at Clarges Street at noon tomorrow in order to propose marriage.

Lady Letitia gripped the tortoiseshell sticks of her fan so tightly that they snapped. In a colourless voice she asked, "Are you sure?"

"Yes," said Jenny, glowing.

"He is too old for you," said Lady Letitia flatly.

"He is very handsome," said Jenny with a defiant toss of her curls. "He is a lord."

"Do you love him?"

"That will come later," said Jenny. "He is everything that is suitable. Come, Aunt. I thought you would have been proud of me."

Lady Letitia turned away. "Yes, yes," she said impatiently. "Do let us leave. I have the headache. Mrs. Freemantle is determined to stay to the bitter end as usual. We shall need to send the carriage back for her."

Jenny tried to talk to her aunt on the road home, but Lady Letitia snapped at her to be quiet.

Lady Letitia slept badly. She was aroused at dawn by the roar of Mrs. Freemantle's voice, shouting from the street below, "Good night, my chucks," followed by a hoarse chorus of masculine voices raised in song.

"She will be foxed again," muttered Lady Letitia, "but I must talk to someone."

This time she went straight down to the kitchen and made the coffee first. But when she pushed open the door of the front parlour, it was empty. She stood, irresolute, and then mounted the stairs and opened the door of Mrs. Freemantle's bedroom.

That lady was lying face down on the bed with all her finery still on, snoring horribly.

Sadly, Lady Letitia turned to walk away, but Mrs. Freemantle gave a last, enormous grunting snore and woke up. "Whash that?" she cried.

"It is I, Letitia. I am s-sorry to have d-disturbed you." Lady Letitia set down the coffee on a table and burst into tears.

"I say! The deuce!" cried Mrs. Freemantle, alarmed into sobriety. "Here, let's have some of that filthy stuff." She tottered over to the coffee-pot, poured herself a cup, and drank the scalding contents in one gulp. "Now," she said, throwing an arm around Lady Letitia's shaking shoulders, "tell Agnes all about it, hey!"

"It's Jenny. She's going to be married."

"And to some adventurer, I'll be bound. Don't worry. We'll send miss back to the country, out of harm's way."

"It's not that. She is to marry Lord Paul Mannering."

"Oh." Mrs. Freemantle sat down on the bed and patted the place beside her and waited until Lady Letitia had sat down as well. "Well," said Mrs. Freemantle cautiously, "he's quite a catch. A gentleman, a lord, and lots of money."

"I am as vain as Jenny," said Lady Letitia, drying her eyes. "You see, I thought he was interested in me."

"Well, you're a fine-looking woman. Plenty of men around."

"But he is the only man I have ever met with whom I have fallen in love."

"Dear, dear. Can't believe that. You must have met someone before."

"I thought I was in love once, but my parents forbade the marriage and I was heart-broken. They said he was a wastrel. I swore never to marry."

"And was he?"

"Yes, as it turned out, they were right. But by that time, I had become in the way of not thinking of marriage, and then I had the care of Jenny."

"You are her aunt. Tell her she can't have him."

"I couldn't do that. If he wants her, then I must be brave. He looked at me in such a way, you know, and all the time he was merely thinking of Jenny."

"She is quite lovely, drat her eyes," said Mrs. Freemantle. "Look, she's bound to oversleep if we don't rouse her. I'll deal with Mannering and make sure he's really serious about this."

"No, I cannot shirk my responsibilities," said Lady Letitia. "I shall see him myself, and, yes, I shall give him my permission."

Jenny did not oversleep. Excitement and anticipation woke her early. Instead of looking forward to Lord Paul's proposal of marriage, she was looking forward instead to telling Mary Maddox all about it. Popular Mary might be, but surely no one had yet proposed to her.

She breakfasted in her room and spent a pleasant morning dressing in her best and having Cooper arrange her hair in one of the latest Greek styles. Rainbird's voice telling her not to look in her glass for a month sounded in her head, but Jenny told herself that she was no longer vain, only glad for Aunt Letitia's sake to have secured an eligible husband.

Her glass told her she had never looked prettier. Little dusky curls rioted from a knot on top of her head, and her fine muslin gown of palest pink embroidered with deeper pink flowers over a slip of white satin was vastly becoming.

Lady Letitia entered just before noon, looking tired and drawn. "You had best wait here, Jenny," she said, "until I give Lord Paul permission to pay his addresses, and then I shall send for you."

"She does look so sad," said Jenny to Cooper when her aunt had left.

"My lady is mortal fond of you," said Cooper. "Her ladyship'll be sad at the thought of losing you."

"Tell me, Cooper," said Jenny, "are there any servants other than yourself and Giles in this house?"

"Why, yes, miss. There are two chambermaids and a housemaid, parlourmaid, and one footman, not to mention the cook and the scullery maid."

"I never see them."

"Mrs. Freemantle thinks it's wrong to keep servants. She thinks we all ought to be able to do for ourselves. So she tells them to keep out of sight at all times—'cept Giles. That way, she can persuade herself she don't have any."

*   *   *

The church clocks were striking twelve when Lord Paul arrived on foot. Lady Letitia stood in the front parlour, holding on to a chair back, facing the door, and waited for him to be announced.

He looked so handsome and so happy that she felt wrenched with jealousy.

Fighting down all these awful feelings, she civilly asked him to be seated.

He looked at her sad, drawn face and some of the happiness left his own.

"Perhaps what I have to say will come as a surprise to you," he began. "I should have spoken to you last night, but after I had gained Miss Sutherland's approval, I found my courage waning, and decided to leave matters until today."

"Not at all," said Lady Letitia politely. "Jenny told me you were to call. You have my permission, my lord."

Happiness glowed on his face. "You accept? I may pay my addresses?"

"Yes, my lord."

"Oh, you make me the happiest of men."

He walked up to her and gently disengaged her clutching hands from the chair back. He slid his arms around her waist and smiled down into her bewildered eyes.

"Oh, Letitia," he said huskily. His lips descended on her own and Lady Letitia found she was being enthusiastically kissed.

Duty fought a raging battle with passion, and duty won. She wrenched herself out of his arms, and backed away.

"May I suggest, my lord," she said, her eyes flashing, "that you keep your kisses for my niece."

He stood stunned. "But that would be most improper, my love."

Lady Letitia sat down suddenly. "Did you not come here today to propose marriage to Jenny?" she asked.

"Of course not!" Lord Paul looked outraged. "It is you I love. How can you think that a man of my years would wish to tie himself up with a little girl? I fell in love with you the first moment I saw you."

"Paul!" Lady Letitia threw herself against his chest and burst into tears.

Upstairs, Jenny began to pace up and down. What could be taking Aunt Letitia so long? Jenny, looking down from the window, had seen Lord Paul arrive. After another ten minutes, she decided to go downstairs and listen at the door of the front parlour.

She pressed her ear against the panels but could hear no sound from within. Anxiety gripped her. Could Lady Letitia, for some reason, have sent Lord Paul away?

Jenny gently opened the door.

Lord Paul and Lady Letitia were enfolded in a passionate embrace. They were lost to the world. Jenny could have screamed or fainted and they would not have been aware of her.

She gently closed the door and stood leaning her back against it, her face quite white.

Then she slowly began to mount the stairs.

Chapter
Six

Whom she refuses, she treats still
With so much sweet behaviour,
That her refusal, through her skill,
Looks almost like a favour.

—William Congreve

It was the worst day of young Jenny's life. She was thoroughly ashamed of herself and made more thoroughly ashamed and miserable when Mrs. Freemantle, on learning the glad news of Lady Letitia's engagement, berated Jenny for having given her aunt so much unnecessary suffering the night before.

Jenny had been much attached to her former governess, Miss Phipps, now living in retirement in Barminster, not realising that lady's slavish admiration of beauty had been a dangerous thing. Everything Jenny did or thought was right in Miss Phipps' eyes. The governess had maintained that any girl as pretty as Jenny did not need to waste her time addling her mind with unnecessary education. Beauty was power, according to Miss Phipps, and beautiful women had a right to use that power to the best advantage because men were selfish beasts and a little teasing and flirting and heart-break never did any of them any harm. Although Jenny had not quite believed the extent of this nonsense, she had formed too high an opinion of her own looks.

Now, once more, she vowed she would no longer consider her own beauty of any great importance. She longed to prove to herself and the world that she was not selfish or heedless. She remembered Palmer again. If only she could do something to help those servants, she would begin to like herself again.

Meanwhile, there was the drive with Mary Maddox and Mr. Toby Parry to be endured.

Mary obviously wondered what was troubling her new friend. She pointed out to Jenny that all the gentlemen were staring at her beauty, but Jenny only gave a little snort and changed the conversation. Her eyes sharpened with misery, Jenny noticed that Mr. Toby Parry was deeply in love with Mary, and that Mary was completely blind to that fact. She also noticed with a sort of wonder that Mary, although highly popular, seemed completely unaware of her own attractions. Perhaps it was more important to have looks like Mary's, thought Jenny, looks that were made appealing and engaging by the very open friendliness of the girl's manner.

"There is your horrible Duke of Pelham," cried Mary, her voice interrupting Jenny's thoughts. "Shall we cut him?"

"No," said Jenny. "A civil nod will be enough, I think."

"Who is that remarkably beautiful creature?" said Lady Bellisle to the duke as Jenny, Mary, and Toby drove past.

"A Miss Jenny Sutherland, but lately come to Town."

The duke wondered what was up with little Miss Sutherland. There had been a certain redness about her eyes that suggested she had been weeping lately, and she looked dejected and miserable. He almost turned his carriage about to go after her, to ask her what was wrong. His conscience gave him a sharp jab. If only he had never said those stupid things about her at Mrs. Bessamy's party. But he decided he had more important business to attend to.

He had visited his lawyers that morning and they had assured him that an investigation into Lady Bellisle's past was not necessary, as, by coincidence, they were her ladyship's lawyers as well. Her husband, Lord Harry Bellisle, had died three years ago, leaving her a fortune. She was very much a lady and had always been so. There was no scandal whatsoever attached to her name.

So the duke decided to get the business of proposing marriage over as soon as possible. He was already bored with the Season. The odd family feeling he had experienced at his town house when he first arrived made him long to retreat to the country and create that atmosphere of home for himself. The fact that Lady Bellisle, who had always lived in Town might not wish to be buried in the country, did not cross his mind. Any lady marrying a duke should have no objections whatsoever.

He was still plagued with a picture of Jenny's sad face, but decided he would put her in the back of his mind until the proposal had been accepted, as it surely must be.

He was about to drive away to a quieter part of the Park when, to his irritation, Lady Bellisle hailed someone in the crowd.

He reined in. "Mr. Frank!" cried Lady Bellisle. "How goes your search for a harlequin?"

"Badly, my lady," said Mr. Frank.

Lady Bellisle introduced the theatre owner to the duke. The duke nodded stiffly, reflecting that the only flaw he could find in Lady Bellisle's character was her absorption in all forms of theatre. From her conversation, he had already gathered she seemed to be on intimate terms with a great number of people in the theatrical profession.

Mr. Frank's shrewd eyes looked up at the duke. So this was Rainbird's master. Now here, surely, was a way to arrange for the duke to be away from his town house for the required length of time.

"But," said Mr. Frank, "I hope to try out a new harlequin tomorrow night. He is a genius. Better than Grimaldi."

Lady Bellisle laughed. "No one is better than Grimaldi."

"I should be honoured if your ladyship and your grace would honour my humble establishment tomorrow night as my guests," said Mr. Frank.

The duke frowned impatiently, but Lady Bellisle turned to him, showing more animation than usual, and pleaded, "Would it not be amusing? Do you care to escort me?"

What else could the cross duke say but "Yes"?

After Mr. Frank had bowed his way backwards as though retreating before royalty, he hurried off to a coffee-house and called for pen, ink, and paper.

He chewed the end of his quill thoughtfully. If he told Rainbird his master was going to be present, then the butler would never put in an appearance. But if he said he had received intelligence that the Duke of Pelham was to be gone from home for the whole length of the performance at some unspecified place and that it was expected to be a small audience at the Spa Theatre, then that might tempt the butler. Pelham would surely sack Rainbird, and that would be all to the good. Mr. Frank was sure Rainbird would be a success. An unemployed butler would be free to take up his new career immediately.

Meanwhile, the duke drove a little way away from the fashionable crowd and reined in his team under the spreading branches of a sycamore tree.

He did wish Lady Bellisle would stop chattering on about the theatre, particularly harlequinades, which the duke considered vulgar.

At last, when she paused for breath, he seized his opportunity.

"I have decided to get married," he said.

She looked at him with a gleam of amusement in her eyes. "Odso! The pretty miss—what is her name?—ah, Miss Sutherland."

"Fustian," said the duke, startled. "Pray why should you think that?"

"I could sense your interest and concern in the girl."

"Miss Sutherland is much too young," said the duke, becoming irritated.

Lady Bellisle looked at him in suprise. "I should estimate the fair Miss Sutherland is nearly twenty, and you yourself, your grace, are nearly thirty. A perfect balance of ages."

"I am interested in a lady of breeding and character," said the duke acidly.

"Oh, I would say Miss Sutherland has those aplenty," said Lady Bellisle with deliberate malice. She had heard the gossip about Pelham's damning of the girl and had decided that Miss Sutherland must have spurned the haughty duke at some time.

"Will you listen to me, madam?" shouted the duke, exasperated.

Lady Bellisle looked at him in amazement, and he coloured faintly. "I apologise for my outburst," he said stiffly. "I fear you are unaware that I am trying, madam, to propose marriage to you."

Those rather protruding eyes of Lady Bellisle's were suddenly hidden as she quickly looked down.

There was a long silence. A light breeze fluttered the sunny leaves above them and flickering shadows dappled their faces. From across the Park came the faint strains of a jaunty march played by the Grenadier Guards. The horses bent their heads and cropped the grass.

"You do not reply," said the duke at last.

"I was waiting for something," said Lady Bellisle.

"I do not understand you."

"It is customary, you know," said Lady Bellisle gently, "to make some sort of protestations of love or affection. That is how it is done. I am used to being proposed to, you see."

"My lady!"

"Oh, yes. I am quite rich and of good family and have no children. Why do you want to marry me?"

"For the reasons you have just stated."

"Well, that is why I am still unmarried. I can afford the luxury of waiting for someone who might love me."

"My lady, whenever did one of us let love enter into the question?"

"I know marriages are usually more like business contracts. My first marriage was such a one. I was quite unhappy, you know, and now I enjoy my freedom."

"I believe you are actually refusing me," said the duke, stunned.

"Yes, Pelham," she said quietly. "That is exactly what I am doing. We should not suit."

"Then I trust I have not embarrassed you."

"Not in the slightest," she said calmly.

He looked at her in anger. The least she could have done, he thought, was to show some regret, some maidenly agitation.

He picked up the reins. "I shall take you home," he said. "The day has become quite chill."

He moved his carriage out into the glare and heat of the sun. Lady Bellisle unfurled her frilled parasol.

"I shall call for you tomorrow," he said stiffly. "At what time does the performance begin?"

"At seven, my lord. But if, under the circumstance, you would rather not . . ."

The duke would definitely most rather not, but he felt it would be churlish and ungracious to say so. "I shall call for you at six-thirty," he said. "What is the play?"

"It is called *The Revenge* or *The Sad Tale of the Miser's Daughter.* After that comes the harlequinade."

The duke thought drearily that the play would probably, as usual, last about five hours, and the harlequinade, one. A total of six hours in an undistinguished theatre in Islington in the company of a lady who did not wish to marry him!

After he had taken her home, he went to his club and there met Lord Paul Mannering and heard the news of that gentleman's engagement.

"I congratulate you," said the duke warmly, looking at his friend's happy face. "I fear you must give me some lessons in how to propose."

"Are you in such need?"

"Alas, yes," said the duke ruefully. "I proposed marriage this afternoon to Lady Bellisle. She appeared suitable. I checked the matter out with my lawyers. She refused!"

Lord Paul surveyed the duke with some amusement. "I think your heart is still whole but your pride is dented. It must have been very embarrassing to be turned down after making protestations of love."

"I made none," said the duke. "I didn't think I had to, you see. Also, that would have been dishonest."

"I am afraid only young misses who must marry will settle for a blunt proposal. Rich widows who enjoy their independence are another matter."

"But Lady Letitia is a rich spinster!"

"Ah, but I love her to distraction. I would not have taken no for an answer. I would have continued to pursue her until she said yes."

"Do you think I am vain and pompous?" asked the duke abruptly.

"Why?"

"I feel vain and pompous."

"Never mind. It must be very hard being a rich duke. Being a rich lord is bad enough. One does get pursued by the ladies so much that when one finally proposes it is natural to expect an acceptance."

"It is such a curst bore," said the duke. "Am I going to have to court one of the creatures?"

"If you do not believe in love, all you have to do is to select a suitable miss and approach her parents. They will accept for her."

"That is what happened to Lady Bellisle, I think. She said she was unhappy in her marriage."

"Quite a number of women are, I believe. But it is their lot."

"'But what man wants to be married to an unhappy woman?" cried the duke.

"Ah, but often he never knows she is unhappy. She must appear all complacency, and is usually happy at first just to be married and to be the envy of her friends. If she is strong-willed, she may take lovers after she is married. You know that to be the case."

"It appeared all so simple," said the duke with a sigh. "Like a military manoeuvre. You select the objective and aim for it. I feel such a fool. Why should I propose to a woman who does not want me?"

"I have always thought you a romantic," said Lord Paul. "Think how disastrous it would be for you to enter into a marriage of arrangement and then find you were in love with someone else!"

"I do not think I am the type of man to fall in love."

"Everyone falls in love at least once."

"I am as bad as Jenny Sutherland," said the duke.

"Lady Letitia's niece! Why?"

"She has become so used to being courted for her beauty that she expects all men to fall at her feet, and I have become so used to toadies and match-making mamas that I, too, think I have only to nod to some female for her to fall into my arms. You must remember, they even followed me to the Peninsula, dragging their daughters along."

Lord Paul smiled. What the duke said was true. Some indomitable matrons thought the rigours of war might prompt a good marriage for one of their daughters if the daughter was on the battlefield, so to speak, and many had succeeded in marrying off plain girls in that way, girls who had failed miserably at their first Season. Lord Paul wondered whether to tell his friend about Jenny having thought his proposal of marriage was meant for her, but loyalty to Lady Letitia kept him silent.

"I trust you and Lady Bellisle parted friends?" he said instead.

"Yes. And now I am promised to escort her to some long and tiresome play at the Spa Theatre in Islington!" The duke laughed. "Do you know, I wanted to shout and rave at her and say, 'Madam, how dare you spurn me! Me, of all people.' But instead I meekly said of course, our arrangement to visit the theatre together still stood."

When the duke arrived home, he asked Rainbird to follow him into the front parlour. Rainbird had received Mr. Frank's letter a bare ten minutes before, Mr. Frank having sent it round by hand.

"I shall be dining at home tonight," said the duke. "Tomorrow night I shall leave about six and be out until late. It is not necessary to wait up for me. There is a change in the air of this house, and I fear it is due to the late hours kept in the servants' hall. Tired servants make unhappy servants. You will see all the staff are in bed at a reasonable hour."

"Yes, your grace."

"Now, send Fergus to me."

When Fergus came in, the duke looked at him impatiently, for his servant was looking tired and sad.

"I am persuaded that no one in this house is getting enough sleep," said the duke, "and that includes you, Fergus. I shall stay at home tonight and tomorrow evening I shall be out late. There is no need for you to accompany me."

Now what, wondered the duke, had he said to make Fergus's face light up, not knowing that Fergus had immediately planned to ask Alice to go out with him the following evening.

"Very good, your grace," said Fergus.

"And see if you can find out if anything is troubling them belowstairs, other than a lack of sleep."

Fergus bowed and went out.

But Fergus's almost constant presence in the servants' hall was why the others could not talk openly. Mrs. Middleton and Angus had planned to announce their engagement as soon as they had gained their freedom. To announce it beforehand would mean Fergus might tell the duke, and as the duke knew that servants were not allowed to marry, he might demand the reason for the odd engagement. Lizzie was nervous and strung up. Mr. Gendreau had given her to the end of the Season to tell the others about her engagement. He had said if she had any free time, then she was to send a note to Manchester Square arranging to meet him. Lizzie was now wondering how she could send that note and was debating whether to take little Dave into her confidence.

She feared Joseph might have sensed something, he was so rude and surly. But Joseph had told Blenkinsop he would take the post as first footman, and, lacking the courage to tell Rainbird, he was unconsciously behaving as badly as possible so as to provoke a quarrel and in the heat of the row bring the whole thing out into the open.

The duke had not told Fergus he was to attend the theatre, and so Rainbird, unaware that his master was to be in the audience, told the others he planned to take Dave out for a walk when the duke was absent. Dave's eyes glowed with excitement, for he guessed Rainbird meant to go to the theatre. Fergus shyly asked Alice to go out walking with him, and promptly went deaf and blind to everything else when she accepted.

Chambermaid Jenny heard Mrs. Middleton saying she and Angus would take a stroll the following evening and offered to go with them. Mrs. Middleton concealed her disappointment very well.

Rainbird went upstairs to stand on the front steps and wonder whether he was being a fool to take such an enormous risk as to face a London audience. He saw Miss Sutherland arriving home and waving goodbye to two friends. Jenny turned to enter the house, but as she did so she looked along the street and saw Rainbird and hurried towards him.

"You should not be seen talking to servants in the street," said Rainbird severely.

"I suppose not," said Jenny, looking not in the slightest concerned. "I heard something the other day about the Duke of Pelham's agent . . . what is his name?"

"Palmer. Jonas Palmer."

"Ah, yes. And he has his offices in the Tottenham Court Road, does he not?"

"No, miss. He's at Twenty-five Holborn."

"How very odd. My friend seems to have heard things all wrong. Thank you, Rainbird."

"What did you hear about Mr. Palmer?"

"You are quite right to reprimand me," said Jenny primly. "I should not be standing here talking to you."

She hurried off and left Rainbird staring after her.

The duke tossed and turned that night, thinking always of Lady Bellisle's rejection of his suit. Was he as romantic as Lord Paul believed? Certainly, his desire to leave his rich and comfortable existence and fight for his country might be construed as romantic. But marriage should be a civilised arrangement, not a turbulent and messy courting full of sighs and sobs such as a person like Miss Jenny Sutherland would surely expect.

And yet she would probably never receive such a blow to her *amour propre* as he had endured. She would finally settle for a suitable gentleman, bear him children, and become placid and fat. He tried to conjure up a picture of a fat Miss Sutherland, but all he could remember was how enchantingly she had danced in the servants' hall and how her curls had tickled his nose.

Two houses away, the object of his thoughts was awake as well. Jenny was turning over in her mind ways to break into Jonas Palmer's office. *If only I had a man to help me,* she thought.

Chapter
Seven

What a parcel of fools and dastards have I nour-
ished in my house, that not one of them will avenge
me of this one upstart clerk!

— King Henry II of England

Various friends of the duke called next day and the staff were kept busy. Rainbird had learned that the duke was to go to the theatre and suffered a momentary stab of fear, but when he asked Fergus whether the duke might by any chance be going to the Spa Theatre in Islington, Fergus had looked surprised and said he was sure his master would not attend such an undistinguished place.

Lizzie, too afraid to take Dave into her confidence in case the pot boy considered it his duty to tell his beloved Rainbird that she was writing notes to a Frenchman, had managed to slip across the street and pay a page who worked in one of the houses opposite to go with her letter to Manchester Square.

At one moment, the front parlour seemed to be full of gentlemen who appeared to have settled in for the whole day, but the next they were gone, and the duke was hurrying into his evening clothes.

The day had been very hot, not bright and brisk and breezy as it had during the previous days, but still and sultry.

The kitchen and servants' hall were like an oven. To add to the misery, the fire in the kitchen had been kept burning all day as Angus had been baking biscuits and cakes for the visitors, and it was now stoked up again to supply cans of water for the duke's bath.

Rainbird said he was leaving. Joseph let out a squawk and pointed out he would need help to empty the duke's bath and carry it downstairs again, but Rainbird did not seem to hear him.

"Are you performing at a children's party, Mr. Rainbird?" asked Lizzie, as she saw Dave slinging the butler's box of tricks, a relic of the days when he used to perform at fairs, up on his shoulder.

"No . . . yes," said Rainbird, and dived up the stairs with Dave at his heels.

All the way over to Islington, Rainbird found himself hoping that the resident harlequin would throw a scene and refuse to stand down, that the rest of the cast would refuse to accept him.

But when he arrived at the Spa Theatre, it was to find that the harlequin was in a drunken stupor and could not have performed anyway, and that the rest of the actors had been warned of his forthcoming performance. He went into a huddle with his fellow actors; Columbine, played by a muscular young man called Jeremy Trip, and Pantaloon, Billy Bright, an old actor with a Falstaffian build. They were to go through the usual pattern of the harlequinade, with which Rainbird, as were most of the British population, was well acquainted. But there were still the long gaps to be filled in by the harlequin with patter and tricks. He asked Mr. Frank if he could have some of the other actors for the opening scene, and Mr. Frank smiled and told him that as long as he did not expect them to learn any lines, he could have as many as he liked.

The evening was so uncomfortably hot that Rainbird kept hoping very few would attend. Surely it would be better to be out in the fresh air on such an evening than sweltering inside this theatre. Rainbird did not know that playbills advertising "The Best Harlequin Since Grimaldi" with the ink still wet on them were being circulated through the streets. Mr. Frank was a gambler and had put a lot of money into getting the playbills out at the last minute. He had even hired two strong men to guard the stage door in case the wrathful Duke of Pelham should try to get to his servant.

As the Duke of Pelham climbed into his carriage, he saw his friend, Lord Paul, emerging from Number 71 with Lady Letitia and Jenny Sutherland. Miss Sutherland stood for a moment on the steps, the folds of her flimsy white gown hanging motionless on her body in the suffocating air. She looked very beautiful and very sad. Lady Letitia and Lord Paul smiled and waved. The duke smiled and waved back. Miss Sutherland gave him a chilly nod, a little dip of the head.

Well, she had no doubt learned of his savaging of her character. He could not expect her to behave otherwise. But her sad face upset him. Had she looked angry and haughty, it would not have bothered him in the slightest. He drove off, trying to put her out of his mind, but he could not help contrasting her present sadness with the happy enjoyment of the girl who had danced in his servants' hall.

Jenny was being taken to yet another Season's engagement, a turtle dinner. She was glad Mrs. Freemantle was going to play cards somewhere else, for Jenny wilted before that robust lady's disapproval. Mrs. Freemantle had not yet forgiven Jenny for having caused her aunt so much unnecessary distress.

As they drove off, Jenny saw the chambermaid Jenny at Number 67, standing at the top of the area steps, and as she looked down from the carriage, prepared to smile, the chambermaid gave her an angry, glowering look before turning around and going downstairs again.

Nobody likes me, thought Jenny Sutherland wretchedly. *Oh, I must see if I can do something for those servants at Sixty-seven. How can I get to Holborn in the dead of night? Even if I wear very plain clothes and try to look like a servant, I shall be in danger of being attacked.*

After turning the problem over in her mind, she said to Lord Paul, "We are fortunate to belong to a class who can afford servants to escort us everywhere. Say some poor girl had to make her way through the streets of London in dead of night, surely she would be in great peril."

"It depends whereabouts in London," said Lord Paul.

"Holborn, say."

"Yes, very dangerous. I would suggest this poor girl of yours save up her pennies for a hack."

Of course, thought Jenny, a hackney carriage was just the thing. She had plenty of pin money left. She would tell the driver to wait for her. Now, all she had to do was hope this tiresome dinner would not last too long.

In Holborn, Jonas Palmer worked over his books. Finally, he threw down his quill pen with a sigh. There was no way he could excuse the bad state of the tenants' cottages on the duke's estates. To put everything in order, even supposing he had the time, would mean paying out of his own pocket. For Palmer had come to consider all the money he had stolen from the duke's estates as his own. He went to a corner of his office and lifted up a loose floorboard and took out the bags of gold he had hidden there and looked at them.

He could buy himself a passage to America and start a new life there. He had enjoyed the power he had had over the duke's dependents more than he had enjoyed getting the money, but he now knew he would be extremely foolish to stay in the country for much longer. He had enjoyed keeping the two sets of books, the real ones showing how he had cleverly managed to feather his own nest. Now, he would have to get rid of them.

He took out one small bag of gold and slid it into his pocket. He would go home and get a good night's sleep. He would book himself a place on the stage-coach to Bristol in the morning and then return, take the gold, and destroy the books.

Joseph minced through the London streets, looking for a breath of cool air. The sun was going down, but the air was still hot and breathless. There was an odd feeling of anticipation in the air, as if the whole large city were holding its breath.

He decided to go to The Running Footman before the heat took any more of the starch out of his cravat. The pub would be hot, but not very much hotter than the scorching streets. He could even feel the heat of the pavements burning through the thin soles of his flat-heeled black pumps.

And then, all at once, he saw Lizzie. She was walking

along on the other side of Oxford Street on the arm of a gentleman. She was wearing her best green gown. She was looking up into the man's face with a silly, doting look—or rather, that was how Joseph described it to himself.

The footman was very angry indeed. Here he had been miserable with guilt at the thought of taking that job with Lord Charteris, and all because he thought Lizzie would be heart-broken. And here she was, obviously the mistress of some foreign-looking gentleman.

"Wait till Rainbird hears about this!" said Joseph aloud, and then glared awfully at a lady who was giggling at him.

A little memory of the old Lizzie who used to look up at him with just such an expression on her face tugged at his heart, and his eyes filled with tears. But he brushed them angrily away, and by the time he had reached The Running Footman, the relief at having a way out of his predicament had banished all sentimentality. He would blame Lizzie's faithlessness for his decision not to join them in the pub venture. That should make the flighty scullery maid suffer every bit as much as she deserved.

"It's just not fair!" said chambermaid Jenny, sitting down on a park bench and bursting into tears. Angus and Mrs. Middleton, who had been walking along in a world of their own, swung about in surprise.

"Whatever do you mean, dear?" asked Mrs. Middleton. The housekeeper sat down on one side of Jenny and the cook on the other.

"I saw her, that other Jenny, that Miss Sutherland, going out for the evening," sobbed the chambermaid, "and it seems wrong that someone with my name should have all the parties and pretty dresses and yet I have nothing to look forward to but a life of servitude. And I'll be alone, mark my words! Alice don't see anything but that Fergus."

She scrubbed her eyes with the back of her hand and glared defiantly at the setting sun.

"But ye're going to be an independent lady. We'll all be free in a few weeks' time," said the cook. "Anyway, God puts us in our appointed stations and it's no use wanting to be a débutante."

"I'll be scrubbing floors and gettin' my hands redder and redder and waiting table. Nothing'll change," said the chambermaid fiercely.

"But ye'll be workin' for yerself," said the cook.

"I'm tired of working," said Jenny with a catch in her voice. "I want to get married."

Mrs. Middleton thought long afterwards that her new status of engaged lady must have activated her brain wonderfully, for in the past she had always turned to Rainbird in time of trouble.

She put a comforting arm about Jenny's shoulders. "I am going to tell you a great secret," she said. "Angus and I are to be married."

"I'm happy for you," said Jenny, gallantly trying to look cheerful.

"I've just had an idea," said the housekeeper, slowly feeling her way. "If Mr. MacGregor has no objection, we will adopt you."

"Here!" cried Angus.

"Yes, adopt you," said Mrs. Middleton firmly. "As our daughter, you would be looked after by us, and we would find suitable young men for you, and you would have the status of the young lady of the house. Your parents are dead, are they not?"

"I s'pose so," said Jenny. "Never knew who they was anyways. But to adopt me!"

"You may have a fine idea there, Mrs. Middleton," said the cook, recovering from his initial surprise. "Aye, I can see mysel' in the part o' the heavy father." He straightened up and glared awfully. "So ye want tae take ma daughter out walking, Mr. Blank? Well, what are your prospects?"

"But what of Alice and Lizzie?" asked Jenny.

"Well, Lizzie has Joseph, and now it looks as if Alice has Fergus. Now you have us," said Mrs. Middleton. "Think, Jenny, it could be fun. Mr. Rainbird says there is not much work to do to put the place in order. Angus is such a superb cook, we shall soon prosper. As our daughter—the daughter of a thriving establishment—you will become much sought after."

Jenny looked at the housekeeper in a dazed way. "And wear pretty gowns?"

"The prettiest we can afford. No more servants' dress. As the daughter of the house, you do not even need to wear an apron."

"Do you really mean it?" asked Jenny, pressing her work-worn hands tightly together.

"Yes," said Mrs. Middleton. "So don't go envying the Miss Jenny Sutherlands of this world. That one will end up like most of the débutantes at the Season—having to take some man her aunt chooses for her. Whereas you will be able to choose whom you please."

"I've never had a mother and father," said Jenny. "Not to know, that is."

"Weel, you have now," said the cook with a grin. "You're a wicked woman, Mrs. Middleton. You've made me a father before I even get ye tae the altar. Come along. This calls for a celebration."

*   *   *

The Duke of Pelham's initial pleasure in finding himself quite at ease in Lady Bellisle's company had begun to wane as the undistinguished play dragged on. At first, he had been relieved that she had seemed to have put his proposal of marriage completely out of her mind. Now he was bored. But his companion did not seem in the least fatigued or exhausted by the long and boring play or by the dreadful heat of the theatre, which was augmented by hundreds and hundreds of candles blazing in a great chandelier overhead.

The play, which was to him pedestrian and cliché'd, appeared to delight her. He began to wonder if the evening would ever end. But at long last, there were the actors taking their bows. The duke clapped dutifully and then half-rose to his feet.

"Your grace!" said Lady Bellisle. "You have forgot. It is the harlequinade with this new harlequin, Rainbird."

He sat back in his chair with a sigh. "I have a butler of that name," he said. He looked at his watch. A harlequinade usually lasted an hour. The effects of his bath had long worn off and he felt gritty, uncomfortable, and hot. It was all very well for the ladies, dressed as they were in near-transparent muslin, but for a man in a starched cravat, waistcoat, tightly tailored coat, and knee breeches, it was hell.

The theatre had been only three-quarters full, but now it was filling up. Everyone wanted to see the new harlequin.

The curtain rose and the audience sat in puzzled silence. It was not like the beginning of any harlequinade they had ever seen. A group of actors dressed as aristocrats sat in a half-circle in a drawing room in front of the fireplace.

which was quite deep. This started the audience laughing and kept them in a good humour.

Someone called to him from the wings, and with a graceful curtsy, Jeremy thankfully made his exit.

The audience cheered as Rainbird came on again. The duke sat forward in his chair and cried, "It is my butler. Wait here, Lady Bellisle. I am going to get that fellow."

"He knows you are here," hissed Lady Bellisle. "He looked right at you. Wait! You can shout at him afterwards all you want, but you are not going to spoil the performance of the best comedian I have seen."

The duke sank back in his chair and glared at Rainbird. If only he had listened to Palmer's warnings about these servants' being Radical. "Radical" was not the word for it. They were mad!

Rainbird was dressed in sober livery. He was carrying a large ledger under each arm.

Mr. Isaacs minced in. "Where are the books, Palmer?"

"I'll kill him," muttered the duke.

"Shhh!" said Lady Bellisle.

"Oh, most noble Duke of Pelham, I have them here," said Rainbird, holding out one ledger and putting the other behind his back.

"He must not find out there is one set of books for me and one for his grace," said Rainbird in an aside to the audience.

The audience began to fidget. This was not very funny.

But then the stage duke demanded the books again, and Rainbird began to juggle them along with the inkwell, a ruler, and a sand-pot. Mr. Isaacs had spent a life improvising. He began to try to catch Rainbird while Rainbird ran hither and thither, still juggling all the objects while the audience began to stamp and cheer.

The brief sketch was quickly over. Rainbird bowed to the audience, and then turned and deliberately bowed to the side box where the duke was sitting.

Then he turned back to the audience and began to regale them with a hilarious description of the news of the day, most of it highly libellous.

The Duke of Pelham sat stunned while his versatile butler pursued Columbine, fought a duel with Pantaloon, juggled and conjured, capered and danced.

"Oh, bravo!" screamed Lady Bellisle at the end. "Bravo!" roared the audience.

"You must introduce me to that wonderful butler," said Lady Bellisle. "What a man!"

"My lady, it is late. I shall deal with the mountebank when he gets home. I shall escort you first."

"Don't be so stuffy, Pelham," said Lady Bellisle. "The man's a genius. Confess. He even made you laugh when he was playing that hussar officer. But it was wicked of him to use your name on the stage. And have you a Palmer who keeps the books?"

"Yes. And the sooner I see him the better!"

The duke drove Lady Bellisle to her home but refused her offer of tea. "Do not be too harsh to that butler," she chided. "He is not a bonded servant, you know. After tonight, I doubt very much if he will ever work as a servant again."

"I am no longer worried about Rainbird," said the duke. "He was trying to tell me that Palmer was fiddling the books. But why he must needs perform it on the stage instead of seeing me in my own parlour any time he cares is beyond me."

After Lady Bellisle had gone in, he set out for Clarges Street, but before he got home, he changed his mind. He drove his carriage down to Lambeth Mews and told one of the grooms to rub down the horses and put the carriage away. Then, tucking a pistol in his pocket, he began to walk through the hot, dark night-time streets in the direction of Holborn. From far away to the west came the low menacing rumble of thunder.

Jenny had been relieved to find Mary Maddox present at the turtle dinner. She did not have much opportunity to talk to her for a long time, as the dinner lasted for five hours. But she was seated next to Mr. Toby Parry and did her best to entertain him. She encouraged him to talk about Mary Maddox and was quite pleased at the end of the dinner to find she had not thought of her own appearance except on two occasions.

She retired to the drawing room with the ladies, and, leaving her aunt to receive felicitations on her engagement, she went to sit with Mary Maddox. To her surprise, Mary was looking downcast, and answered all Jenny's questions in monosyllables.

Jenny was about to give up and walk away and find more pleasant company when she decided that the new Jenny would surely stay put and try to find out what was ailing Mary Maddox.

"I think," she said firmly, "that if we are to be friends, there should be frankness between us. I must, therefore, ask you, Mary, why you are so sad and why you so obviously wish me in Jericho."

Then Jenny waited bravely for the reply. What if this newfound friend should say something awful, like "It is because you are so vain."

Mary gave a little sigh. "It is hard not to be beautiful,"

she said in a low voice. "Everyone loves you when you are beautiful. I wish I looked like you."

"But since I came to London, everyone seems to be telling me I ought to be like you," said Jenny. "All talk of the openness and charm of your manner."

"Nothing compared to beauty," said Mary sadly. "I have never before seen Mr. Parry look so relaxed or happy as he was this evening in your company."

"You widgeon!" cried Jenny. "I know the way to that young man's heart. I talked about you!"

"Me?"

"Yes, *you,* silly. I knew poor Mr. Parry was deeply interested in you, but I thought that you were not interested in him."

Mary seized Jenny's hands and held them in a tight clasp. "You are not funning?"

"Not I. I talked about you and asked questions about you, and any time I looked like changing the subject, he lost interest."

When they were joined by the gentlemen, Jenny had the joy of seeing Mary's happiness as she sat and talked to Toby Parry. It was a wonderful feeling to have been instrumental in bringing happiness into someone else's life. During the dinner, Jenny had half made up her mind not to go to Holborn.

But now she was more determined than ever.

Chapter
Eight

A man that studieth revenge keeps his own wounds
green.

—Francis Bacon

Jenny had been very pleased with her appearance before she slipped out of the house after Lady Letitia had gone to sleep. She had wrenched all the feathers and ornaments from a straw bonnet and reduced it to a modest shape. She was wearing a simple morning gown and she had wrapped an old shawl of her late mother's around her shoulders. Looking in the glass before she left, she was reassured by her dowdy appearance. Rich clothes would have attracted too much attention.

But the Jehu on the box of the hackney carriage which she hailed in Piccadilly looked down doubtfully at the drabness of her dress and demanded his fare in advance.

"Very well," said Jenny crossly, handing him a shilling. "But you must wait for me."

The coachman grunted by way of reply, and Jenny climbed into the malodorous interior of the carriage. She jerked the carriage window down, but the air that poured in was far from fresh. London smelled appallingly of bad drains and horse manure.

The rattling of the old carriage prevented her from hearing the approaching storm.

So she was surprised by a tremendous crack of thunder almost overhead when she alighted in Holborn. The horses reared and plunged. "You will wait?" she called up to the coachman.

"You ain't paid the way back, miss," he called down, "and I'm gettin' out of here afore the storm breaks."

To Jenny's great irritation, he drove off.

Well, really, she thought crossly. *Now I shall just have to find another when my business is done.*

The door from the street into the building was unlocked. She twisted the knob and let herself in and mounted the worn shallow stone steps, feeling her way upwards. Why had she not brought a lantern or a candle? But such an important person as the duke's agent would not lodge in the attics. She waited on the first-floor landing until a great flash of lightning struck a brass plate beside a mahogany door. PELHAM ESTATES leapt out at her in a sudden glare of gold before the stairwell was plunged into darkness again.

Here I am, thought Jenny, now terrified out of her wits. She began to wonder whether madness ran in the Sutherland family. What on earth was she doing, standing on a Holborn staircase in the middle of a thunderstorm? But there was no one around, and she could not possibly leave until the storm had abated. She squared her shoulders, took a deep breath, and tried the door handle. The door was tightly locked.

Jenny had never really worked out how she was going

to get into the agent's office. She stood and looked at the door in a baffled sort of way. Then she remembered reading a romance where the heroine had picked the lock of her dank dungeon with a hairpin. She fished in her reticule and brought out a bone pin and set to work.

Above her the storm increased in fury, and the very building seemed to rock beneath the onslaught. Her fiddlings and probings had no effect whatsoever. But the heroine of the book had taken half an hour over the business. Jenny bent her head and tried harder than ever. Between her intense concentration and the noise of the storm, she did not hear footsteps behind her as someone mounted the stairs.

The Duke of Pelham saw the small, dark, anonymous figure stooped over the lock. He mounted the last stairs in a bound and seized Jenny roughly and turned her about.

"Who are you? What the deuce do you think you're doing?" he grated.

Jenny screamed and punched at the white blur of the face above her own. Another great flash of lightning lit up the stairwell.

The duke dropped his arms to his sides. "Miss Sutherland!" he cried. "What on earth are you doing here?"

"Pelham. Oh dear," said Jenny. "Must I tell you?"

"Of course."

"I came to aid your servants. I cannot tell you who told me, but they believe your agent is cheating you and feel sure if they found the accounts books, they could prove the matter."

"Am I such a monster that they cannot come to me in mine own house and voice their doubts?"

"But don't you see," said Jenny eagerly, "it might turn out that you are the skinflint and not this Palmer."

"I am tired of all this nonsense. Return to your carriage and maid, Miss Sutherland, and do not interfere again in my affairs."

"But I cannot," wailed Jenny. "I did not bring my maid, and the hackney carriage would not wait for me."

"Then come along and I shall take you back."

"Are you not going to open the door?"

"I intended to shoot open the lock. I cannot do that with you fainting and screaming."

"I shall not faint and scream," said Jenny, anger at the duke bringing all her courage back.

"All ladies faint and scream at the sound of shots. Oh, very well. Stand back. I shall wait for the next crack of thunder. I do not want the neighbours to call the watch."

Jenny retreated a little. There was a brilliant stab of lightning, then silence. Then a preparatory rumble and a tremendous explosion as the duke shot the lock in the middle of the noise of the next thunderclap.

"The deuce," she heard him mutter. "Stay clear, Miss Sutherland. That was only one lock. I have to shoot the other."

Again they waited. Far above them, rain drummed down on the roof.

Then came the lightning again. Jenny put her fingers in her ears this time.

The duke's timing was wrong and the shot rang out before the thunderclap came.

He stood for a moment listening, and then he kicked open the door.

Jenny went in after him. She heard the rasp of a tinder-box and then an oil-lamp on Palmer's desk bloomed into yellow light.

The duke raised the lamp and looked at Jenny. Despite

the drabness of her dress, she made a romantic figure with her dark curls rioting from beneath her bonnet. Her large eyes looked black in the whiteness of her face.

"Sit down," said the duke, "and bend your head down towards the floor. I have enough to do without having to trouble myself restoring you from a faint."

"You are rude and pompous, as I told you before," said Jenny, stamping her foot. "I am not going to faint."

"Then find a chair, sit down, and keep quiet. How convenient. My agent has already been at his books."

The duke sat down at the agent's desk, pulled the lamp close, and began to read.

Jenny studied him. He was very handsome. Such a pity he was a churlish brute, she told herself huffily. She waited and waited, and yawned and yawned. "You might at least tell me," she said at last, "whether your agent is an honest man or not."

"Far from honest," said the duke. "Those servants at Clarges Street must have been living on their wits, else they would be skin and bone now on what he paid them. But why did not Rainbird tell me? Why cavort around the public stage?"

"Rainbird the butler? What do you mean?"

"I went to the Spa Theatre at Islington tonight with Lady Bellisle. To my amazement, my butler was acting the part of harlequin. He also acted the part of Palmer and did a mime of trying to keep the books from his master. That is why I came straight here when the performance was over."

"Are you going to marry Lady Bellisle?" asked Jenny.

"Miss Sutherland. We have broken into a London office in the middle of the night. You are unchaperoned. And yet you find time to ask trivial questions to satisfy your idle curiosity!"

Jenny blushed and looked away. Her eye fell on a loose floorboard in the corner. She rose to her feet.

"Where are you going?" asked the duke.

"There is a loose floorboard over there," said Jenny. "Perhaps Palmer has sacks and sacks of gold underneath it."

"If you ladies would stop addling your heads with Mrs. Radcliffe's romances, it might . . . Leave that floorboard alone. It is a loose floorboard, nothing more."

But Jenny had slipped her fingers under the end and lifted it up.

Then she bent down and pulled out a wash leather bag and opened it.

"Here you are!" she cried triumphantly. "All your money. Perhaps if you addled your own brains a little, your grace, you might not be so stuffy and narrow-minded."

The duke crossed over and knelt down on the floor and began to take bags of gold out, one after the other.

"Apologise!" cried Jenny.

He knelt silently looking at the gold.

"Apologise," said Jenny again, and she gave his shoulder a shake.

He twisted round and looked up at her. Her eyes were full of mocking laughter, her shawl had slipped from her shoulders, and as she bent over him, he could see the shadowy swell of her breasts revealed by the low neckline of her gown.

He gazed at her, his eyes suddenly serious and intent. A huge burst of thunder cascaded down over their heads.

He reached up and took her by the shoulders and pulled her down until she was kneeling in front of him.

138

"I am very stupid," he said. "I never notice what is under my nose."

"You mean Palmer?" asked Jenny, her eyes wide and wondering.

"No," he said softly. "I mean you."

His hands slid to her waist. "Jenny," he said softly.

"Oh, no," said Jenny. "Not you. You, of all people."

He frowned. "And what do you mean by that?"

"I thought you would be too formal and stuffy to take advantage of me. I know my behaviour this evening has been disgraceful, but it does not mean my morals have been in the slightest damaged."

"Stop talking. I want to kiss you."

"You cannot kiss me. You have not asked Aunt Letitia leave to pay your addresses to me."

"I' faith, I did not say I wanted to marry you, only to kiss you."

"Then you cannot have kisses without marriage, and I don't want to marry you."

The fact that Lady Bellisle had not wanted to marry him had wounded his pride and irritated him, but nothing more. But Jenny's saying she did not want to marry him caused him a stab of acute anguish. He looked at Jenny in dawning amazement—amazement that such a little chit should already have the power to inflict such pain on him.

The only way he could think to ease that pain was to kiss her.

And so he did.

And he went on kissing her, uncaring of the blows she was raining on his chest. His kisses were gentle, serious, passionate, and intent. Jenny decided wildly that if she stopped fighting him, and lay limp in his arms as if she had fainted, he would soon stop. But before he raised his mouth from hers, her body had already begun to respond in a dreadful way. The minute she found herself free, she should have leapt to her feet. But instead, her arms seemed to wind themselves about his neck of their own accord, and her lips blindly sought his.

After some time, he untied the ribbons of her bonnet and pulled it from her head, and then buried his lips in her hair.

The very noise and fury of the storm, combined with their passions, kept all thought of the conventions at bay. It was only kissing. No amount of thunder and lightning would make the duke forget himself as much as that. But the kisses became more dragging, more lingering, sweeter to the point of pain.

He was stretched out beside her on the floor, her hands were buried in the crisp golden curls at the nape of his neck, his hands were moulding her face, when a harsh voice called, "What's this 'ere?"

The duke sprang to his feet and Jenny scrambled up after him.

The watch, accompanied by the parish constable, were standing in the doorway.

"There is no need for alarm," said the duke haughtily. "I am Pelham."

"And I am the Archbishop o' Canterbury," sneered the watch. "Firing pistols in the night and frightening the neighbours. It's off to the round-house with you and your doxy, my fine sir!"

Before the storm broke, there had already been a feeling of friction and tension in the servants' hall, as if an emotional storm were slowly approaching from the west, borne on the black thunder-clouds covering London.

Joseph was racked with a mixture of spite and guilt. Perhaps if they had all gone to bed at a reasonable time, matters would have remained the way they were for a little longer. But Rainbird was still absent, and they were all waiting for the butler and Dave and wondering what had become of them.

"They would probably have heard the thunder and have gone somewhere for shelter," said Mrs. Middleton. At that moment, a great white light flashed into the servants' hall as the lighting stabbed down overhead. Mrs. Middleton screamed. Then there was a great crack of thunder.

"Oh, Angus!" cried Mrs. Middleton. "It sounds like the end of the world!"

"There, now," said the cook. "I'm here, my good lady. There is nothing to fright you."

He put an arm about her shoulders and Mrs. Middleton forgot herself so much as to lean against him and smile up into his face.

"What's this?" cried Joseph. "A-kissing and canoodling like a pair o' love-birds. Seems to me, Mr. Rainbird'll have something to say about this."

"Leave the good lady alone and mind your own business, young man," said Fergus quietly. He covered Alice's hand with his own, and Alice blushed and looked down.

"This is what I get for all my loyalty," shouted Joseph. "Everyone's smelling of April and May, 'cept Lizzie, who prefers to sell her body."

Angus crossed the kitchen and jerked the footman to his feet by his cravat.

"I've a guid mind tae wash your mouth out with soap," he said.

"It's true," said Joseph. "Ask her. Ask Lizzie who she was with in Oxford Street tonight. Oh, we're going to get the pub, ain't we? And we're all going to live happily ever after, ain't we? Mrs. Middleton will marry Rainbird and I'll marry Lizzie and we'll all be one big happy family in that poxy, tumbledown pub in the country. Pah! Ask her where she's been and what's she's been doin' of."

Angus made a noise of disgust and let the footman go. Mrs. Middelton said quietly, "Lizzie! What is all this about?"

"I was going to tell you," said Lizzie. "I didn't have the courage before. I am going to be married."

"Married? To whom?"

"To a Mr. Paul Gendreau. He was the Comte St. Bertin's valet. But the comte died and left him money."

"And you fell for it," jeered Joseph. "Whenever did a valet with money marry the likes of you?"

"He is going to marry me," shouted Lizzie. "And I'm going away and I am not going to the pub. So there!"

"And I'm not going to that pub neither, then," yelled Joseph. "I'm going to be the Charteris' first footman. And it's all on account o' you, Lizzie. I knew you was playing me false."

"You don't care for me one bit," said Lizzie. "Not one little bit! All you care about's yourself, you great popinjay."

Incensed, Joseph slapped Lizzie across the face. With a growl, the cook fell on Joseph and the pair rolled over on the floor, Angus punching and Joseph screaming and kicking and gouging.

The door opened and Rainbird walked in, followed by Dave. He jumped on the two fighters and tried to pull them apart, calling to Fergus for help. At last Joseph and Angus were separated.

"What is going on?" demanded Rainbird, seizing a towel and wiping the rain-water from his face.

An angry babble of voices answered him.

"One at a time," said the butler, sitting down. His eyes went over their faces. "You first, Mrs. Middleton."

"I am to marry Angus MacGregor, Mr. Rainbird," said Mrs. Middleton.

Joseph's malicious eyes darted eagerly to the butler's face, waiting to see it contorted in anger, but to his surprise, Rainbird looking immensely relieved. The butler rose to his feet, raised Mrs. Middleton's hand to his lips, and kissed it.

"All happiness to you both," he said. "This is a cause for celebration, not fighting. Now, what started the trouble? Lizzie?"

Lizzie, tearful and defiant, told the story of her engagement.

"Well, be it a respectable offer, then I am happy for you," said Rainbird quietly. "But why did this Gendreau fellow not call on me?"

"Because of the pub," said Lizzie wretchedly. "I hadn't the courage to say I would not be going with you."

"Then you must tell him to call on me tomorrow—today," amended Rainbird with a glance at the clock. "You have no family but us, Lizzie, and you need someone to interview this gentleman for you."

"She was promised to me," said Joseph. "You know that."

"It was understood, yes," said Rainbird. "But I never thought you would suit."

"What!" screeched Joseph, sounding like a parrot getting its tail feathers pulled.

"And Joseph is not going with us either," said Mrs. Middleton. "He is to be first footman for Lord Charteris."

"So Blenkinsop got after you, did he?" said Rainbird.

"How can you think of going on being a servant when freedom is at hand, Joseph?"

Everyone had forgotten that the intently listening Fergus was not supposed to know about their future.

"I' was on account of Lizzie being unfaithful to me," said Joseph sulkily.

"The real truth, Joseph," said Rainbird sharply.

"S'welp me Gawd . . ."

"Joseph!"

"Well, I didn't want to go to the country," muttered Joseph. "There's nothing there for a fellow to do. All horses and sheep and cows and smelly animals like that. Waiting on table in ordinary dress. No livery."

"But our livery is a very sign of our servitude!"

"You may think what you like about your'n," said Joseph hotly, "but I look very fine in mine . . . when it's brushed and pressed, that is, and hasn't been mauled around by some Scotch barbarian."

"Enough, Joseph," chided Rainbird, seeing the cook was ready to return to the battle. "So now we have a situation where neither Lizzie nor Joseph will be with us . . . or . . . ?"

He cocked his head and looked inquisitively at Alice, who sat hand in hand with Fergus.

"I must speak to my master first," said Fergus. "But I have asked Alice if she will be willing to have me and she has said yes. I cannot marry without his grace's permission, but I trust he will find me employ as perhaps a keeper on one of his estates. He can be very haughty, but he has never been so with me. And since he has been here, I have detected a softening in his attitude to others."

"But you could always join our venture," said Mrs. Middleton.

"Perhaps," said Fergus. But the jealous Fergus wanted Alice all to himself and did not want to share her with these servants, who, he feared, might turn out to behave towards him in the manner of so many mothers-in-law.

"And Jenny?" asked Rainbird.

"Angus and I are going to adopt Jenny," said Mrs. Middleton. "Now that Lizzie and Alice are settled, it would only be fair to give our Jenny the position of daughter of the house."

The others cheered and laughed at the idea, telling the chambermaid that Angus would have her speaking Gaelic in no time at all. Only Joseph sat silent. No one had screamed or protested at his going. No one wanted to adopt him—not that he wanted a quiz like Angus MacGregor for a father.

"Aye, it's going to be me and Mrs. Middleton and Jenny with Mr. Rainbird and Dave to run the pub," said Angus.

"No," said Rainbird quietly.

Unable to contain himself any longer, Dave burst into speech. "Mr. Rainbird's goin' on the stage, wiff me to help him. We're goin' to be ever so rich. Strewth! You should ha' seen that audience tonight laugh and cheer and the Duke o' Pelham hisself right in the side box watchin' Mr. Rainbird act the part o' Palmer, juggling the books."

Rainbird was immediately surrounded by them all, demanding to know what Dave was talking about. He told them about his performance and of how he had decided to show up Palmer on the stage.

When all the exclamations and questions had died down, Fergus said, "Why did you not tell my master of your suspicions?"

"Because," said Rainbird, "when I listened at the door

to him talking to Palmer, he seemed surprised at the paucity of our wages but not as shocked as he should be. I do not know him well and feared he might prove clutch-fisted."

"Not his grace," said Fergus loyally. "He is often cold and indifferent-seeming with both servants and soldiers, and yet he always treats them fairly and looks out for their welfare. Me, he has treated more as a friend than servant. I have never had reason to complain of the money he pays me."

"But can we afford to run this pub now?" asked Mrs. Middleton. "Alice and Lizzie will need dowries. Joseph will keep his share of the money, as will you and Dave."

"You can keep mine," said Rainbird, "and Dave's. We talked about it on the way back."

"Mr. Gendreau told me I need no dowry," said Lizzie. "So you can have mine."

"Provided his grace agrees to my marriage and sets me up in some capacity," added Fergus, "then I do not wish a dowry from Alice."

"What's that hammering at the door!" cried Rainbird, starting up.

He ran up the back stairs, followed by Joseph, Angus, and Fergus.

A member of the Horse Patrol stood on the steps, instantly recognisable as such by his blue greatcoat, black leather hat, and scarlet waistcoat.

"There's a swell cove locked up in the round-house with his moll what says he's the Duke o' Pelham. He says if his man, Fergus, comes along, he can vouch for his identity."

"We will all go," said Rainbird. "It must be the duke himself, for he is not yet returned."

All the momentous things that had happened in the servants' hall, all the changes in their future plans had kept everyone over-excited. The ladies would not consider being left behind.

So, to the Horse Patrol officer's amazement, it was a whole household of servants who walked behind his horse as he led them through the rain-washed streets to the round-house. Far above the twisted, jumbled chimneys, the thunder gave a last menacing grumble, and the stars shone in a clear sky.

The Duke of Pelham thought he would never get free, even after the arrival of his servants. Everyone was shouting explanations. Miss Jenny Sutherland had so far forgotten herself as to run from one servant to another, hugging them and calling them "the best of people," and telling them that Palmer had indeed been cheating the duke.

When he was finally borne out of the round-house at the front of the little crowd, it was to find that Rainbird had every intention of going straight to Palmer's lodgings and confronting him.

"When you identified me, I immediately ordered Palmer's arrest," said the duke wearily. "Leave the matter to the authorities. I found all the money he had stolen from me."

"*I* found it!" said Jenny hotly. "You would never have found it by yourself. Oh, do let us go, Pelham, and see the end to the story."

She was hanging on his arm and smiling up into his face. His heart gave a lurch. "Very well," he said weakly. He turned to Rainbird. "But immediately we get home, I want an explanation from you."

Palmer lived in lodgings off Oxford Circus. But by the time they got there, the agent had already fled. A man who lived in the attics above his office, who had heard the shot and alerted the constable, had run round to Palmer's lodgings to tell him that an impostor calling himself the Duke of Pelham had been arrested. From his description of the "impostor," Palmer knew the game was up. For if the duke had shot open the office door instead of waiting to see him in the morning, then it was certain the duke had somehow found out about his, Palmer's, trickery.

"Let us try the coaching stations," cried Rainbird.

"No, leave it be," said the duke. "The authorities will find him if he can be found."

They meekly obeyed him this time, and they all set out on foot for Clarges Street.

It was a silent group. Rainbird knew he was going to have an unpleasant interview; Fergus dreaded the duke's possibly refusing to give him a post that would allow him to marry.

Jenny was blushing all over as she thought of her own behaviour in Palmer's office. All that time in the roundhouse, the duke had not said one word of love, only raged up and down demanding their release.

"Everyone into the front parlour," said the duke when they reached Number 67. "And let's get to the bottom of this."

Jenny stood back a little. He seemed to have forgotten her existence. She felt she should go home and yet knew she would not sleep unless he smiled at her just once more or showed some sign that he cared for her, if only a little.

At first the duke found it hard to make out what it was all about as everyone started to talk at once. They were going to buy a pub; the chambermaid was crying out that she was the cook's daughter; the footman was screeching that Lizzie had betrayed him; and Fergus was beseeching him for the post of gamekeeper or some other employment that would allow him to marry as soon as possible.

But at last, they all quietened down, and he heard the story from the beginning. "But why did Palmer claim he paid you low wages—even if they were in fact higher than the ones you actually got? He could have fleeced me for more," said the duke at one point.

"It was because, I think," said Rainbird, "that he did not wish to bring the running of this house too much to your attention. He could explain away the low rent for the house, for this house is reported to be unlucky, and people were too superstitious to pay a good rent for it. But if you noticed that you were keeping a whole staff of servants all year round at reasonable wages, then you might have inquired further. Palmer enjoyed the power he had over us. He enjoyed our misery and seeing us starve. That was more important to him than any money. He cheated you in this respect out of a matter of habit."

"He was certainly taking enough from me in other ways," said the duke, "but never too much. Most of the gold I—we—found had been accumulated over the years, I think. He was clever enough not to be too greedy. You are not the only servants who were paid low wages, although none fared as badly as you. I had meant to review all the wages when the Season was over. I shall give you a sum of money towards your pub to make up for what you have suffered. Now, is there any more?"

There was. Another half hour passed while Rainbird explained his theatrical career, and Fergus begged to marry Alice.

"This is all too much," said the duke, clutching his golden curls. "Yes, Fergus. I shall find you something close to me, for I do not wish to lose you." He turned to Angus

149

MacGregor. "So it appears you and Mrs. Middleton are to have the running of this pub. Do you think you can be successful? Is the building in good repair?"

"I havenae seen it, your grace," said Angus. "Mr. Rainbird bought it for us. We were not planning to leave you until the end of the Season. We have not had time to go to Highgate."

"You may go now, if you wish," said the duke. "You may all consider yourselves free. But I would suggest we all get some sleep."

But that word "free" had made all their dreams—with the exception of Joseph's—a reality.

"Why not now?" said Mrs. Middleton boldly. "I could not sleep. We could go now. See, it is light already."

"Miss Sutherland," said the duke, looking at her tired face, "please go. Tell Lady Letitia I shall call on her."

"Take me with you," said Jenny suddenly to Mrs. Middleton. "Take me to see this pub." Jenny was afraid to let her time with these servants end, for fear it would mean an end to her time with the Duke of Pelham.

"Miss Sutherland, Lady Letitia will be alarmed to find you not in your bed. She may even be looking for you."

"I could tell her I had gone out driving with you, Pelham . . . " said Jenny.

"At six in the morning?" said the duke. "Nonsense."

"Oh, I see," said Jenny sadly. A scarlet blush coloured her face and she looked at her hands.

The alarmed duke realised in a flash that Jenny thought he had kissed her for a whim and now wished to forget about the whole thing. And he didn't.

He wanted to kiss her again. He wanted to make sure he had her all to himself before another man in London saw her. But dukes did not go to Highgate with their servants to look at a pub after a night in the round-house. Dukes did not . . .

Jenny's lip trembled.

"This is idiotic," he said, "but I suppose we could leave a note for your aunt explaining the situation. Yes, we will all go to Highgate!"

That redoubtable female, Mrs. Freemantle, arrived home at dawn as usual and stood on the steps of Number 71, swaying slightly, and waving drunkenly to the party of young men who had escorted her home. She unlocked the door, tripped over the threshold and stretched her length in the hall. The tiles of the floor were beautifully cool and she was just closing her eyes to settle down for a short nap when she saw a letter lying just beside her head. She picked it up and rolled over on her back, cracked open the heavy seal, and squinted up at it.

"Pelham," she murmured. "Gone to a pub in Highgate with Jenny . . . calling later to ask permission to pay his addresses . . . drat, this must be for Letitia." She tossed the letter on one side and closed her eyes. Her feet, encased in bronze kid Roman sandals, were sticking out onto the doorstep; her turban had fallen from her head. A light breeze moved through the coarse hairs of her scarlet wig.

But before she could drift off to sleep, the full impact of what she had just read blazed in letters of fire across her brain.

"The deuce!" she screamed, leaping to her feet. "Letitia! Letitia!" She staggered to the stairs and managed to run up four of them before swaying helplessly like a person on a tightrope and falling back down again.

By crawling on her hands and knees, hauling herself up the staircase as if scaling a mountain in the Alps, she finally reached the second floor. She drew a great breath. "Letitia!" she shouted.

Lady Letitia came out of her bedroom, looking dazed and alarmed.

"Pelham's going to marry Jenny," said Mrs. Freemantle, and then hiccupped.

"Of course he is," said Lady Letitia soothingly. Mrs. Freemantle, who had been on all fours, slid forward onto her face and went to sleep.

"Oh dear," said Lady Letitia. "I do not know how Agnes can consume such quantities of wine and stay alive. I shall get the coffee-pot before I try to get her to bed."

She returned to her room for a wrapper and then made her way downstairs to find the street door wide open and a letter addressed to herself with the seal broken drifting across the tiled floor on the morning breeze.

Lady Letitia carried the letter down to the kitchen, stoked up the fire, swung a kettle on the idle back, and then rested one hip on the kitchen table and read the letter.

"Oh, my goodness," she said. She ran from the kitchen and up the stairs again, calling "Agnes!" at the top of her voice.

When they arose that morning, Mrs. Freemantle's servants grumbled to find the kettle boiled dry and a hole burnt in the bottom of it.

Chapter Nine

A little work, a little play,
To keep us going—and so, good-day!

A little warmth, a little light,
Of love's bestowing—and so, good-night!

A little fun, to match the sorrow
Of each day's growing—and so, good-morrow!

A little trust that when we die
We reap our sowing! and so—good-bye!

—George Du Maurier

It was two carriage loads that set out for Highgate as the birds began to twitter on the roof-tops and the rain dried from the streets.

Somehow the duke did not find it at all odd when someone, he did not know who, suggested they go via Manchester Square, where Mr. Gendreau still resided while he waited for his late master's affairs to be wound up.

Rainbird, still slightly worried by Joseph's malice, was relieved to meet the sober and pleasant French valet.

Joseph was not. His livery was still dusty from his fight on the kitchen floor with Angus, and a purple bruise on his temple was beginning to throb. He felt the others were disloyal in the hearty, friendly way they greeted this French valet, this frog, and Lizzie's behaviour was quite disgusting. They had all let him down, thought Joseph, quite forgetting that he had wanted to go to Lord Charteris's household anyway.

Miss Jenny Sutherland sat beside the duke in his phaeton. The rest of the party were crammed into the duke's travelling carriage, following behind. She wanted to look up into his face to see whether he was angry with her but did not dare. What had he written to her aunt? Had he asked leave to pay his addresses, or had he put it some other way? He had said he did not want to marry her, only to kiss her. But then surely she had a right to ask what he had written.

She cleared her throat, feeling so nervous that she wondered whether her voice would sound normal or whether it would come out in a frightened squeak. She did not know whether she loved the duke or not. She only knew she could not bear the idea of his loving anyone other than herself. She remembered Lady Bellisle and her heart sank.

"Pelham," she ventured.

"Yes, Miss Sutherland?"

That was a bad start. If he had said, "Yes, my love," or even, "Yes, Jenny," either would have been so much more encouraging.

She gulped and stared unseeingly out at the New Road Nursery and did not find the courage to say anything further until they had entered Pancras Road on the other side of Islington Street on their road north to Highgate.

"What did you write to my aunt?" she eventually asked.

"I wrote to explain that I was taking you on a drive to Highgate."

"And that was all?"

No, it had not been all, and the duke knew it. All he had to do was to tell Miss Sutherland that her aunt expected a visit from him later in the day when he would ask Lady Letitia's permission to pay his addresses to Jenny. But what if Jenny refused him? What if she had only kissed him back out of fear? He racked his brains, but could only remember his own great passion. How was it that he who had faced so many battles without a qualm should quail before the very idea of being refused by this one débutante?

"No, it was not all," he said. He let the reins drop and his horses slowed their pace. The carriage with the servants passed them and Dave, perched up on the roof with Rainbird, blew a cheeky blast on a yard of tin.

"I told Lady Letitia," he said in a neutral sort of voice, "that I would be calling later in the day."

"Aunt Letitia will certainly expect an explanation," said Jenny. "She will think it most odd that I went out driving with you at dawn without consulting her, and she will want to know when we made such an arrangement."

"Yes, I realise that."

Jenny peeped up at him hopefully, but he was looking straight ahead. He looked grand and remote. He had changed into morning dress. His blue swallow-tail coat, white cravat, and curly-brimmed beaver seemed so respectable compared to her own dowdy gown and shawl. Her bonnet, for all she knew, was still lying on the floor of the agent's office. She should have gone home to change while he was changing but had feared discovery.

"And what explanation will you give Aunt Letitia?"

He reined in the horses and turned to the sad little figure beside him in his phaeton.

"I shall tell her simply that I love you and want to marry you. With any luck such news will drive all questions about this outing from her mind. I feel I have compromised you and must marry you."

"Then I shall lie and lie about last night," said Jenny. "I shall never marry any man just because he feels obliged and constrained to do so."

"This is silly," said the duke. He caught her in his arms and began to kiss her fiercely. "Do you love me?" he asked at last.

"Oh yes," said Jenny. "I really think I do." He fell to kissing her again while his horses looked over their shoulders in surprise.

Only the raucous jeers of a passing cartload of market workers brought him to his senses. "We had better catch up with the others," he said reluctantly, "or I shall spend hours around Highgate looking for this pub. Hold on tightly. I'm going to spring them."

Jenny grasped the side of the phaeton as they began to race through the streets and out into the countryside. She felt dizzy with happiness, felt like shouting aloud as fields and trees and bushes flew past.

They soon caught up with the others. The duke slowed his hectic pace, and they made a decorous passage through Highgate village and on to the pub on the other side.

"What's that, Joseph?" asked the cook as they all walked into the inn after Rainbird had unlocked the door. The footman was carrying a large cardboard box with air holes punched in the sides.

"It's the Moocher," said Joseph.

The Moocher was the kitchen cat, a great striped tiger of an animal, and Joseph's pet.

"What are you bringing it here for?" asked the cook.

"'Cos I can't take it to my new job," said Joseph, lifting the large cat out and placing it on his knee. "You'll need to take care of it and be kind to it 'cos it's the only one in the whole wide world what loves me." Joseph buried his face in the cat's fur and began to sob.

The duke, Jenny, Fergus, and Paul Gendreau looked on as the servants all crowded around Joseph.

"We all love you, Joseph," said Mrs. Middleton. "Don't stay in service. Come with us. We'll adopt you too."

Angus stifled a groan.

"Listen, Joseph," said Rainbird. "You know you accepted Blenkinsop's offer before you knew what was going to happen to the rest of us. You want Lizzie to stay the same, running after you and listening to your every word, but you don't want her to marry you. But if the idea of working as a first footman is making you so miserable, then don't. Do as Mrs. Middleton suggests and stay here."

Joseph dried his eyes and looked cautiously round the circle of faces. Lizzie's eyes were swimming with tears. The Moocher put its paws on Joseph's shoulders and stared into his eyes with an unblinking glare.

The footman remembered that Blenkinsop had said he was to wear a special new scarlet-and-gold livery and he was to have a spun glass wig and would not even have to worry about powdering his hair. The very thought of such finery sent a warm glow into Joseph's heart. The heavy cat gave a faint miaow. Joseph looked again at Lizzie, and the better part of his nature came briefly to the fore.

"I'm sorry," he said. "You have the right of it, Rainbird. I really do want that job. Don't cry, Lizzie. Only promise you'll come and see me sometimes."

"I promise," said Lizzie softly while Mr. Gendreau looked on and thought it would be a long time before he allowed Lizzie near this popinjay of a footman.

"That's that, then," said Rainbird. "Let's look around."

The duke and Jenny went off into the garden to sit by the weedy pond and to leave them to go over the pub from attics to cellar.

"Are all servants thus?" asked the duke.

"No," said Jenny. "Their hardships have drawn them very close together."

"What shall I do with Fergus? He will need a house and some sort of position."

"Why not give him the horrible Palmer's job?" asked Jenny. "I am sure someone could train him to keep the books and then you would always be sure of an honest agent."

He stood up and picked her up in his arms and then sat down again with her on his knee. "You are going to make me a very good wife," he murmured against her hair. "Fergus shall be my agent. You have brains in your pretty head. And to think I thought you vain!"

"And to think I thought you pompous," said Jenny. Then she frowned. "But, you know, I think I was very vain and I do think you were pompous. The house in Clarges Street is said to be haunted. Perhaps it is haunted by good ghosts who change people for the better."

But she could not discuss the matter further for he had started to kiss her again.

*   *   *

Lady Letitia and Mrs. Freemantle were shocked out of their wits when they came upon the entwined couple in the inn garden.

"Disgraceful, Pelham!" boomed Mrs. Freemantle.

The duke and Jenny stood up, hand in hand.

"You may congratulate us," said the duke. "We are to be married."

"I should think so too," said Mrs. Freemantle before Lady Letitia could speak. "Frightening us out of our wits and forcing us to rush out here after you. Tell us, Pelham, how it transpires that you and Jenny are here in a run-down inn with servants? Tell us why you saw fit to go out driving at dawn?"

"Sit down, ladies," said the duke. "It is a long story."

The sun rose higher in the sky as he told his tale. To Jenny's relief, the shock left both ladies' faces as the bizarre events were recounted. Mrs. Freemantle was highly entertained, and Lady Letitia thought the couple's adventures had brought about a much-needed change in both.

Then Rainbird came into the garden to announce they had been into the village to buy food and drink for luncheon. They carried tables into the garden and soon they were all enjoying an al-fresco meal while the Moocher rolled in the grass at their feet in the sun.

All the couples were toasted. The duke, mellow with happiness, smiled at Angus. "Tell me, MacGregor," he said, "what would you and Mrs. Middleton like as a wedding present?"

"Dogs," said the cook. "I would like thae dogs."

"Dogs? What dogs? Are there dogs in my house?"

Angus MacGregor shook his fiery head. "I mean the two iron dogs chained on the doorstep. When times was bad, I felt like one o' thae dogs. I have a mind to have them on the doorstep here."

"Then the dogs are yours. Do you stay on here? Am I now temporarily without servants?"

"We will stay for another week," said Rainbird, looking questioningly at the others, who all nodded.

"Good. That will give me time to make other arrangements."

The sun was going down in the sky before they all set out for London.

When they reached Clarges Street, the duke said goodbye to Jenny, promising to call for her in the morning as early as possible. Mr. Gendreau drew Lizzie aside. "I do not like leaving you with that fellow, Joseph."

"Joseph's all right," said Lizzie. "I love Joseph still, but I am not in love with him. Can you understand that?"

The tactful Mr. Gendreau nodded, although he did not understand it at all. He disliked Joseph intensely, but he knew if he voiced his dislike, he would make Lizzie unhappy. Better to bide his time for a week and then snatch her away and keep her too busy to go running back to Clarges Street.

He contented himself by drawing her behind the duke's travelling carriage and kissing her for the first time. That kiss was all he had hoped and dreamt it would be, and Lizzie's dazed and happy face allayed his jealous fears about Joseph.

As Fergus prepared his master for bed, both heard the jaunty playing of Joseph's mandolin filtering up from the basement.

"Do they never sleep?" yawned the duke. "We will talk tomorrow, Fergus. I have plans for you."

"Yes, your grace. May I have your permission to retire?"

"Meaning, may you go straight downstairs and join the rest? Yes, Fergus."

Fergus ran downstairs. They were all grouped about the table in the servants' hall. Alice was laughing at Rainbird, who was singing a comic song to Joseph's accompaniment. Fergus felt a stab of jealousy. Alice was too close to these people. She was not even related to any of them. He picked up a chair and squeezed his way in between Alice and Angus and possessively took her hand, feeling all the time like an interloper.

The Season was finished. Society followed the Prince Regent to Brighton. Jenny, Lady Letitia, and the duke had gone to the duke's large mansion in Shropshire to begin preparations for two weddings. Lady Letitia was to marry Lord Paul from the duke's country home a week before Jenny was to marry the duke.

Lizzie had married Mr. Gendreau by special licence, and they had moved to a house near Bath, having bought one as close to the house of their dreams as possible.

Alice and Fergus had gone with the duke to his home and were to be married in his private chapel one week after his own wedding.

Angus MacGregor and Mrs. Middleton had been married before any of them had left. It was the last gathering of the servants of Number 67 before they split up, and they were all there to wave goodbye to Angus and the new Mrs. MacGregor and the soon-to-be Miss Jenny MacGregor.

Rainbird was now playing to packed houses in the provinces, with Dave on hand to manage his affairs and carry his props.

Resplendent in his new livery, Joseph was the envy of the servants at The Running Footman. He was having a certain difficulty fending off the amorous approaches of his mistress, but felt sure he could continue to cope with this problem. The servants in the Charteris household treated Joseph with all the respect due to the position of first footman, and Joseph only occasionally felt sad when he walked past the shuttered windows of Number 67 and saw the empty places on the front steps where the two iron dogs had stood.

Jonas Palmer sat sulkily in the heaving nightmare that was the ship bearing him to America. He could not believe life could be so unfair. After he had reached Bristol, his pocket had been picked. As he was a wanted man, he dared not go to the authorities. But he also dared not remain in England. There was only one way a man without money could get a free passage to America.

So Jonas Palmer, bonded servant, was on his way to Philadelphia, where he would have to work for seven years for no wages whatsoever. He blamed it all on Rainbird; he felt sure it was the butler who had found out his guilty secret and reported it to the duke. He often thought of Rainbird and hoped the duke had thrown him out and the butler was starving to death.

Lizzie Gendreau put down the letter she had been reading and blushed guiltily as her husband came into the room.

She had finally achieved the proper status of a lady. At first, it had been very difficult managing her own servants and accepting her new status, but with a year of marriage nearly over, she had almost forgotten what she had felt like in those early days when she had first gone to Clarges Street as a scullery maid.

"Who has been writing to you?" asked her husband.

"It's from Mrs. MacGregor," said Lizzie. "You remember, she was Mrs. Middleton, the housekeeper. She thought it would be a famous idea if we had a reunion in a month's time—at the inn."

"And no doubt that coxcomb, Joseph, will be there?"

"Yes. But you must know you have nothing to fear from Joseph, and I would so like to see them all again."

He looked at her pleading face. "Very well," he said softly. "I shall take you there and leave you with them for one day, but that is all. I shall come in the evening to fetch you."

And so the former servants of Number 67 all made their way on a June evening to The Holly Bush in Highgate. It was odd to think that, after all their long discussions about names for their pub, the MacGregors should have done nothing about changing it from The Holly Bush.

The pub had been closed for the whole day in honour of the reunion. They talked and talked. There was so much news to exchange. Joseph was more refined than ever and full of London Society gossip. The former chambermaid, now Jenny MacGregor, was shortly to be married to a local farmer. Alice was pregnant. Rainbird had gone from success to success, and Dave was very finely dressed and apt to put on airs. Angus told them all the dramas of their first year and bragged how his cooking now drew people from far and wide and that they were going to hire builders to turn the place into a posting-house. Joseph took out his mandolin and played the old songs. But by evening, the visitors were growing restless and anxious to be on their way.

"It'll never be the same," mourned Joseph as he stood outside with Lizzie. "We was all so close once."

"We all grew up, Joseph," said Lizzie softly. "And you are happy, aren't you?"

"Yes," said Joseph. "Yes, I am." He looked down at the chained dogs on the inn steps. "To think o' the number of times I polished them things," he said.

The air was soft and warm and the birds chirped sleepily in the ivy on the walls of the inn.

"I'm happy for you, Lizzie," said Joseph. "You're a real lady now."

On a sudden impulse, he hugged her close.

Paul Gendreau, arriving at that moment in a gig, made no comment, but he vowed, as he had once before, that it would be a long time before his wife was allowed to see her old companions again.

Rainbird drove Joseph back to Town in his spanking-new carriage and set the footman down in Clarges Street.

"See you very soon, Joseph," he called. "See you very, very soon. We'll all meet again."

Joseph stood and watched until Rainbird's carriage had turned the corner of Piccadilly.

He went to enter Number 69, but instead, he turned about and went and stood outside Number 67 and looked down at the dark basement.

He felt something important had gone out of his life. He found himself gripping the railings and wishing the candles would light up that darkness and Rainbird's voice would be raised summoning him to his duties.

He went sadly into Number 69 and down to the servants' hall.

"Good evening, Mr. Joseph," said a blushing housemaid. "We was just about to have supper."

"Thank you, Amy," said Joseph loftily. He sat down next to Blenkinsop and snapped his fingers as a signal that he was to be served.